MACHINE GODS
OF THE
ETERNAL SEA

MACHINE GODS OF THE ETERNAL SEA

By

Terry Lee Smith Jr.

Illustrations By

Terry Lee Smith Jr.

Order this book online at www.trafford.com
or email orders@trafford.com

Most Trafford titles are also available at major online book retailers.

Illustrations By Terry Lee Smith Jr.

Printed in the United States of America.

ISBN: 978-1-4669-0922-9 (sc)
ISBN: 978-1-4669-0923-6 (e)

Trafford rev. 01/20/2012

 www.trafford.com

North America & international
toll-free: 1 888 232 4444 (USA & Canada)
phone: 250 383 6864 ✦ fax: 812 355 4082

CONTENTS

I would like to recognize and thank my family
for their continual support.

MACHINE GODS OF THE ETERNAL SEA

CHAPTER 1

In the beginning, man has learned many things. He has walked through its deserts and forests. His domain has become all he sees. And yet he is still the same. This is the point man has reached; growing beyond his own triumphs through rugged hands to a pure simplified thought. It is a far era where human kind has consistently built over civilizations of the past. We are at a place where just about anything is possible. A time where the Devil's promise in Eden of man's own mastery of himself into a God is close to fulfillment. Or furthest away.

As it was told in a passage about history: Through the ashes of a once barbaric era did the people of the Earth form into one grand unification known as the Nations of Earth. Afterwards little time has passed when mankind became masters of time and dimensional rifts; cutting their way beyond space and reality by departing shuttles known as Systems Shuttles. These large ships are what brought the people of Earth closer than they have ever been to the rich universe. We rose through the heavens where life can be more fruitful on worlds as barren and empty as Hell or as lushly and more exotic than the Earth itself.

A century passed when an explosion of population grew on thousands of habitable worlds swept forth. Everywhere there was an industrial revolution unlike ever before that in fact benefited the leaders of Earth all the while the "Mother World" itself underwent an environmental change for the better.

But what is our place? Like an unsuspecting seed did man grow from simplicity to a raging inferno in his Master's "Garden." Spreading forth and fulfilling his destiny to bring about the beginning of the end.

The Nations of Earth have traveled to and studied thousands of systems. They held the majority of suitable worlds as colonies as the rest were ignored for their overly volatile or unlivable conditions. Those were unique times to be alive as for the first time world traveling and colonization for over generations became simple.

Yet it is not as simple to say that peace and tranquility was always a given under the Nations of Earth. In fact the

Mother World knew that such an expansion throughout many solar systems required a strict govern of laws and control directly under the Nations of Earth. As a law, very few systems have lords or representatives of their own choosing apart from Earth. The only exceptions are worlds that lie on the sheer outskirts of the known universe and take the furthest to reach in case of an emergency. All other systems were governed by the Nations of Earth. No Lord or colony could form their own government or military strength apart from Earth's. And in doing so would be considered a threat to the Mother World and dealt with swiftly. And even with no new systems allowed to be controlled without the Nations of Earth's consent, still a large percentage of the gross economy, industry, and population to those worlds outweighed the Earth and its forces. Thus a powder keg was set.

War would soon gallop on the heels of a spoken word: Independence. It was also the ideals of repression and a wide spread feeling of disassociation from the world that birth all original human life. The Nations of Earth failed to show themselves as fellow citizens or neighbors to the universe. But how could they? Colonist issues were not the same as Earth's as they proved to be the laborers born without a spoken word of their own.

Soon a wildfire of fear spread from the strength and iron fist of what the colonists considered to be the corruption of the Nations of Earth. Next generation war machines walked and surprisingly ascended to the heavens and space. With their faces gleaming of metallic iron, they await in formation to unleash the dogs of war from their masters' grip. From every battleship to colony they are legion; towering high above the innocence below.

"Did you know, Miss Kempt that it is exactly 129 years After Ascension?"

"Yes, General. I hear some places are celebrating."

"Yes," said the General, "still celebrating despite all that has happened." Miss Kempt replies off course, "I have the results on the subject, General Armada." The gray haired General pauses in thought, clasping his wrinkled and veiny hands low. "How is the boy?" he asked. Miss Kempt answers coldly with eyes low on a chart she is holding, "Stable." "Good." said Armada. "That will be all Lieutenant." As she begins to walk away towards a dark hall, General Armada begins to look on down through a very wide double plated glass.

He remains undisturbed in the cold and gray room alone yet never feeling vulnerable with the hint of alcohol under his breath; warming his veins. And down below in a sarcophagus-like chamber sleeps a young teenage boy. He is very gaunt in appearance with his bare chest exposed. An over-head light can be seen flooding down on him; darkening all surroundings. His eyes twitch and clasp roughly every so many timed seconds as if having a controlled nightmare. "Sleep . . ." hushed the General. "Sleep well, Cero."

He sleeps the impossible dreams of the past. They are dreams that are not his own. Force fed images of Earth tyranny on the freedom hungry colonists of the newly founded Devoir Con-Systems. He dreams of a twisted and maniacal idealist's vision of what could and will be. Cero was abandoned and found in the wake of death and destruction like so many infants during a war that had lasted for 20 years. Within his sleep he sees himself presently as a 14 year old boy walking through the ashes of a city street. Forever trudging that familiar mile.

With legs feeling as heavy as steel, Cero continues past the visibly dead that scream quietly a sound he can only imagine with their mouths open to an awful blight. Cero bares no expression as a dark colossal iron giant glares its dark crimson eye before his presence. Coming forth from the fire, it stretches out its metal gauntlet; twisting its almost live gears and tendons at the boy. Swiftly it is met with a churning and fiery billow of black debris that screeches and volleys about Cero; dying out the red eye.

Looking above, Cero witnesses a more awesome sight. In the distance a warm glow cannot escape his vision even as he shuts his blue eyes. And though Cero has been on this bloody field before, this thing is something new to him. Something that is more confusing and frightening than ever before. He is seeing the birth of a second sun that is falling and then expanding before the city's outline in the far distance. Soon those very outlines are consumed into that very glow; coming ever closer to Cero. As a common fear rushes through his veins coldly, he falls to both knees in a hopeless effort to brace what is to come.

A single tear can be seen rolling down his cheek all the while his mind fills with voices. Voices that tell how to survive by fighting a war in another time and another place. Voices that tell to not fear the end for Cero is the creator of this. Prerecorded voices that say: Love in me for I am your General.

Large Inbound Experimental (x) Unit Fighter: Iron Dragon
Xiston Special Unit 0, Code Named: Cero

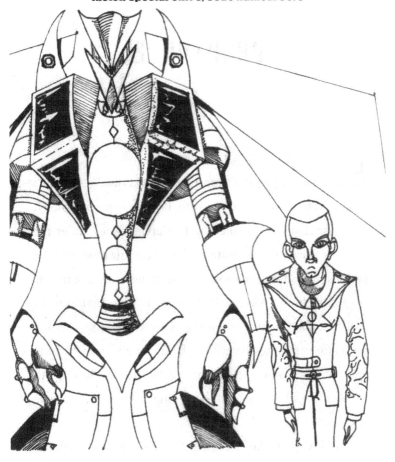

MACHINE GODS OF THE ETERNAL SEA

CHAPTER 2

HERE LIES THE planet Xiston. Or what is known as Armada's Xiston. The planet Xiston, with its single moon known as Lunar Xiston, was ruled by 12 Capital Cities under the Nations of Earth for a century since its colonization with the first Capital City named Soul. As one of the wealthiest worlds controlled by the Mother World it had a rich environment that sustained natural resources. Xiston was once a strong blood flow into the heart of Earth. Yet it never fully became an aristocrat's world. It was an "of the people" world. But no one could imagine it becoming a more militaristic stronghold.

A few years later during the 20 years war, eleven pre-emptive nuclear attacks nearly ended the people of Xiston's reality until they were occupied by Devoir forces.

They were brought on by Devoir from space. The battle above and around Xiston was futile for the Earth forces there as they were surprised by Devoir's brutality. Xiston was an example of pure chaos as those on the ground were shown no mercy under the metal boot of Devoir. The first and only nuclear attacks came before civilians could relocate safely. As a result, many families were displaced; some to never see each other again.

Xiston was then manned as a platform and thus used as a major role against the Nations of Earth. Eventually a Systems Pact was agreed on in which Xiston remained as a Devoir Con world. The long and bloody war had ended. But there Xiston lies. Forever riddled with the visible scars of a brutal and savage change. The only last capital city to survive through the nuclear-curtain was Soul. And though Soul was spared, the planet was left as a mere shell of itself.

Some of the people of Xiston felt abandoned while many others accepted and honored the Con-Systems' Lords who maintained their way of life and helped in restoring cities. Xiston had to except a Nationalist. A General named Armada was chosen by the Pride Systems personally as a direct representative of Devoir.

What Devoir destroyed was rebuilt along with the thoughts and will of the people. Propaganda was sold into Xiston's heart by Armada of a false idea of tomorrow which gave the civilians a false hope in his competence as a leader. Their will allowed General Armada to carry out his secret agendas as he pleased.

A peace amongst all worlds has lasted for nine years. Nine years of peace. Nine years of Devoir preparation and planning. Xiston is stead-fast in pivoting as the most lucratively armed and heavily defended world; unrecognized by the Nations of Earth. And the General does have plans for not just Xiston but all of Devoir Con.

General Armada is in his quarters sitting at his ridged desk. He has a dark glass in one hand and an old file in the other. It is a sixteen page file on the on-goings of Xiston prior to the war. Dust about him swirls naked to his eyes. He had this file for quite some time. Armada takes a sip from the unrecognizable sauce that hugs his lips so. General Armada had this file for nine years. It makes sense to him to focus on something that is there rather than nothing at all. His room is bare except for his desk, a coat rack, and a bed and bathroom in two separate rooms closed by doors. Perhaps the General has gotten rid of most things useless to him. It is the things he believes he needs most of all are what he wants; and in doing so he searches for that at the bottom of his glass. Occasionally he finds himself actually skimming through the file before feeling the need to take another drink.

Little time passed when a young woman stopped short of his door and pressed a button on its paneling; triggering a low monotone chime. The General, finding himself in mid drinking, quickly places the glass on his desk. "It's open." he said loudly. There was a time when he would have hid his glass from whoever bothered him to attend his duties and responsibilities.

He keeps his stern face cocked at the door. She walks at attention before the front of his desk. It's a Sergeant "someone or other," according to him, that is below Lieutenant Kempt. "The experimental unit is ready for its last testing, sir." she said bluntly. Armada keeps a very limited staff under his direct wing. But no temptress of a woman could ever claw as close to him as he allows Kempt to be. Armada thinks of reassigning some of the women from his staff.

"Why interrupt me with a frivolous thing, Sergeant?" barked the General. "Can't you see I was in the middle of something-" "Sir, it was your direct order to inform you on the project's final go." she tiresomely interrupted. Armada squints his hawk eyes and answers, "I see . . . and understand. You're excused." General Armada stands up and grabs his officer coat from the rack while watching the Sergeant shuffle off. He pauses in mid thought and wonders: Has it really been nine years?

Leaving out he turns to where there are elevators. As he enters within he presses for first level. It has barely occurred to him that he is ten levels below sea level. The General dwells within the core of this living base. Its walls are more alive with the blood of the planet Xiston and the secrets of a future hell-bent on reshaping the universe forever. And it has been quite some time serving within this mega complex known as the Artificial Island Base and Defense-1.

It's a super base, fully armed as a planetary defense against invading fleets from space. But more importantly it serves as a covert platform for experimental soldiers and unit fighters.

The General's mind swirls and wades smoothly from the motion of the elevator's force and the drink he had a little earlier. With his eyes closed he thinks that no place could ever make a prison more unbearable than his own mind. General Armada's presence on Xiston was seen by him as his destiny. His past is only known by a still living few. The very man is in fact convinced his presence is the sole face of Devoir. And his soldiers or experiments here are the key to everything. Finally he reaches his destination. A light chime signals off before the elevator door opens.

It was a short walk past technicians, engineers, and the like when Armada comes to a personnel platform where Lieutenant Kempt stands while staring out into the cold northern Xiston oceans. With the entire base in the middle of an ocean, on it, Armada finds himself with Kempt outside and below two upper decks. They are within a lighter armored and exposed portion of the base.

The General remains behind her to adjust his arms from out of his coat's sleeves in order to put them underneath it for more warmth. Occasionally the wind would blow more flurries of snow towards their direction; coming forth and away. Kempt just leaned her figure towards the railing to adjust. General Armada took her beautiful womanly stance in for a moment. That was one of the things he liked most about her. He often thought that perhaps in his younger days . . .

He searches feverishly within his coat's inner pockets for something other than a flask. Stepping forth he pulls out two cigarettes past her shoulder. She takes one and begins to light it from a lighter in her own pocket. Lieutenant Kempt knows he would have wanted more out of her. She often thought he would want to make something else out of her. Armada lights his with his personal gold flip lighter. "So this is it?" asked Lieutenant Kempt. She takes a long smoke which allows the red glow to eat away at the cigarette faster. He answers, "For the fate of one world . . . Yes." Armada takes in a harder but shorter puff.

"The fate of one in order to save many others." exclaimed Kempt. "Then you understand completely, Lieutenant." said Armada. She gives half a glance of her face, locking an eye with Armada and smiles as warmly as she could against the cold weather. Looking away, she further leans against the iron sturdy structure; allowing the wind to sift through her hair. "So where is he?" asked General Armada. "On the very top deck. He'll be going through some final preparations before taking off." said Kempt. Not long now do the two feel a slight rumble. Armada, due to his age, grabs onto the Lieutenant's shoulder to steady himself. He knows the power he is about to feel. Finally they are met by an awesome jolt followed by heat from above that warms them to their core. Suddenly there is a lulling hush followed by a tremendous engine outflow screech. Both the Lieutenant and General shield their eyes with their arms to only scantly witness a titanic, bipedal Unit Fighter soar 45 degrees up from their perch. The only lasting colors are primarily of an aged blood stained red.

Greedily, Armada couldn't keep his gaze from the dusk sky. The northern Xiston seas themselves couldn't keep him from the prize. Armada can't see the beauty in anything anymore. The landscape couldn't be painted more serene or peaceful. It was lost to him through battle and despair many years ago. Yet frightening to any outsider; he is hopeful.

It's thin compared to other unit fighters. But its lighter armor keeps it fast. Unlike any other fighter its mechanics and mobility are determined by the flexibilities and thoughts of its pilot. Along with new large external shields on both of its sides, Armada's latest X-Unit has no rival. "The Devil's Son." said General Armada. "That's what we're calling it." Caught in mid inhale of her cigarette, Kempt holds it until her eyes feel misty. After exhaling a large puff, she says, "Cero should be ready, sir." "Good." answered Armada. "We shouldn't waste any time, Susan." Lieutenant Kempt tosses her cigarette over and into the ocean waters. Quietly she leaves Armada who doesn't notice her with his eyes to the sky.

High above the artificial island, the Devil's Son waits. The experimental unit fighter utilizes all of its stability thrusters against Xiston's gravity. And surprisingly it remains as still as a mountain. Compared to most unit fighters, the Devil's Son stands out with three head attachments. Though large, two are on both sides of the head; curling downward. The third is placed on top and just over a little over the head. All of which serve mysterious purposes. Yet the most striking features are its shields that drape like a cape as if for show. They glare colors of blue, red, and green. Lacking mostly any armor, this fighter's presence or vibe can't help but to feel an eerie shutter within.

The General continues to watch as several glints from the horizon appear. He knows they are Unit Drones guided by an artificial intelligent system. They are older Nations of Earth Unit Fighters that have been captured and re-outfitted. These hulking masses are practically rusted and are of no use but fodder. Now they are represented as the enemies of tomorrow; brutishly armed with external guns in tow, missile locked within shoulder hangar stores, and out dated internal mechanisms.

The Devil's Son quickly powers up its forward thrusters before boosting off towards the drones at a fantastic speed. One of the drones levels off to engage. It is a classic maneuver. As the Devil's Son crosses through the other drones' formation, its pilot merely flips a switch to turn its stealth capabilities on thus leaving the unmanned "armors" in disarray. Though this is an upper hand in battle by hindering monitor and targeting capabilities of its enemies, that doesn't stop the lone drone from getting a visual.

After firing round after round seemingly forever with its right arm held ballistic assault rifle, the Devil's Son's shields activate. Every shot fired is absorbed before the X-Unit. And with a wave of its gauntlet, the Devil's Son fires a shotgun blast of bolted and charged energy. An energy almost like the one projected from its shields.

While the drone's beating follows its shattering destruction, the large debris from its black and mid-air explosion forces it to fall in large pieces. The drone's parts make a very high and loud splash. Its descent into the icy waters alerts the other hungry drones.

As if full of vengeance, one fires a single missile that trails towards the crimson warrior. The Devil's Son merely dodges it with its gauntlet poised at the drones. At a closer glance by the drones' AI real time camera they can see that the gauntlet finger tips are hollow. And within are that which fired again at another drone . . . Fortunately for the drone it was a clear miss. Coming ever closer to the Devil's Son, the X-Unit's pilot gets suicidal "snapshots" of the zooming drones and wastes no time in positioning himself for another kill.

Surprisingly the drones turn their torsos towards the Devil's Son while disengaging their forward thrust; relying solely on momentum. Their on board tracking relies on an old historical gun sight as they each open fire on the X-Unit. The Devil's Son defiantly boosts forward through the melee. It dodges left from right before coming upon its next victim. A stream of charged energy cuts through and maims the drone's chest armor which causes it to spin away and down into its icy tomb.

As another drone sizes the moment of opportunity, it boosts forward as if wanting to make an assured shot. After firing just a few rounds that hopelessly absorb, the Devil's Son pushes the drone closer to it by grappling it with its large gauntlet fingers. A unit fighter that is as flexible as the Devil's Son which can grab on to another is awesomely unique.

The last drone launches a barrage of missiles that track swiftly to the pair. The X-Unit fighter pushes the hapless drone away with its armored knee. The explosion ripples the waters below; leaving behind nothing but fiery falling debris.

The Devil's Son stares down the final one. With one armored arm up, targeting the drone, it charges its weapon to the fullest for one lasting shot . . . It went quickly as the last to fall. For once in a long time, Armada is pleased. But deep within the artificial island base it is Lieutenant Kempt who is bent on having the final say. And it is for the sake of all mankind.

As she walks into the now lit area where Cero sleeps, Kempt realizes the rest of the staff have already exited with Cero just ready to awaken. Indeed Susan Kempt, under the devil Armada himself, is a covert agent under the Xiston Ecologist Faction. Ironically they consider themselves soldiers against war. And these latest events proved Devoir Con to be the enemy of peace. But in all wars there are sacrifices. Because Susan has gotten this close to the General's on-goings and malicious plans, Kempt was assigned to influence Cero to be a covert soldier to the Ecologist Factions. And to prove to General Armada that he is incapable of fighting.

But time and time again Susan could see that she failed with her own brain subjugation of Cero that remains undetected by Armada and his hand-picked staff. Lieutenant Kempt proved herself to be good but it just wasn't enough. She remembers her last subjugation ordered by the Ecologists was something of their "ideal" humanity. None the less her job is to continue her work.

She was given orders by her covert superiors to check her contact point for further instructions. This time it is an old waste basket with a small note inside. It was obvious to her that it was left by a faceless contact. Some time ago she heard that the contact is a traitor to Devoir. Walking over to the basket, she picks up the single note. Susan nearly drops to her knees; shaking a bit. Dropping the note beside her, Susan finds herself beginning to sob softly. As if to cover the shame of her despair she bangs the side of a lab table harshly and says, "Those damn fools!"

The note is a direct order concerning Cero: Protocol-Alpha-Execute-Zero. It is a direct order from the highest level to kill Cero. At this point all Susan can think is: Hypocrites, all of them!

She is far from thinking of when and where to do the indecent deed. Even so she is feeling ill about the mere idea. "To kill a boy?!" she said softly to herself. "How could they-" Cero awakens; shuffling about in his open chamber. The boy couldn't help but look about. He finally sees Kempt. She is a very familiar face to him. Though he is only 14 he has always had a sixth sense about people and Kempt was always pleasant around him. She even revealed her first name to him once. But now she seems to be distraught. His disciplinary training prohibits him from speaking when not spoken to. Cero's cold blue eyes rarely asked of anything from any authority figure but his mind could not help from wondering static questions of why or how.

"Good. You're up." said Susan while adjusting her clothes and hair. She is ignoring any ill feelings as well. What most don't know about Susan Kempt is that she has the know-how to destroy half the island base with smuggled explosions if the execution order was given. The Ecologist Faction would expect nothing less.

She walks over to him as Cero lays flat into his chamber while being ever so tense. She notices and asks, "Didn't they ever teach you 'at ease?'" Susan smiles warmly as Cero didn't seem to get the joke. Very rarely did Cero see anyone smile since he could remember except for Susan. She shines a light in his eyes than orders, "Sit up."

Lieutenant Kempt now checks the wired cerebral feed in the back of his neck that runs down into his chamber. Strangely Susan has a hard time focusing on anything but the short haired boy. She could do it now, she thought. Just be done with it. Susan unhooks the cords gently with a slight tug. Susan is smarter than that and she knows it. She thinks with a smile to it all, I'll have none of it! She gives Cero a wicked smile.

Susan reaches down below where a flat drawer opens from the chamber. A pile of neatly folded clothes waits. "Get dressed." said the Lieutenant. He straps out of the chamber and very quickly fits about the dress pants, under shirt, over coat, and shined black shoes. His belt fits tight and strict, or better said more appropriate for a funeral. The colors are typically Devoir Con attire with a striking yellow Pride Systems' insignia on his over coat on top of the black and grays.

Kempt bends down to Cero and gets in close to his stern face. She says to him softly, "You're, err, you were always like a son to me. Do you . . . understand? For what it's worth . . ." She kisses him on the cheek more softly than anything he has ever experienced in the fourteen years he's been under General Armada. In fact it hasn't occurred to him what a kiss is. She pauses, forgetting who they've made him become. A soldier. "Take care of yourself, Cero." she continued. "Stay alive."

General Armada stumbles in drunk with joy over the final testing of the experimental unit fighter: The Devil's Son. A near outburst of laughter misses escaping his throat when he sees Cero all buttoned up and standing in attention. Attention for the glory of *his* Xiston.

Cero's and Susan's eyes are met with confusion in seeing Armada nearly knocking over lab equipment. "You there, Cero, my boy . . ." he said while picking a flask out from under his coat to his less than dry lips. "You're going to change everything! The whole thing." "Sir?" questioned Susan Kempt as she stands protectively close to Cero. "Susan," he said in one harsh gulp, "is he ready to launch in the Systems Shuttle?" Lieutenant Kempt answers, "Yes sir. And his specific unit fighter is within the same shuttle, ready to launch on your go." "Good. Then now our boy shall remember his code name: Cero." said Armada walking closer to Susan and Cero. "The world out there is different, my boy. No simulation or training will prepare you for what you'll see, smell, or even do. But I trust in you as I do all my soldiers . . ."

Armada stops short of Cero. What he said about soldiers made him think about the others like him on the island base. Their chambers reside on the far right wall. All empty except for one. "Our sufferings," he dragged on, "our sufferings are almost at an end. And we're at the pinnacle beginning of a new."

Neither Susan nor Cero could possibly understand the full intent on Armada's rambling. But Susan knows he is the hand or catalyst in representing Devoir's agenda: To once again ignite the battle flag of war against the Nations of Earth. And as for Cero, his thought is on keeping his promise to Susan: To stay alive.

MACHINE GODS
OF THE
ETERNAL SEA

CHAPTER 3

H<small>E DISTURBS HIS</small> sheets from his side of the bed. His dark skin further masks his feverish writhing within the dark and crampt room. The bed, as soft as civilian-possible, he cannot feel. Sweat trickles through his braided hair. His name is Troy Arlington. Troy is dreaming a true nightmare of the wicked ways of men. It is a nightmare of the once living past 20 year war for the planet Rhim. The historic "Battle for Rhim" was a mad man's vicious paradise. Human life feeding on human life was both of the beasts' desire. And those like Arlington were the teeth.

Troy Arlington first began an interest in piloting unit fighters at a young age as a result of a strong military upbringing. It was during the beginning of the 20 year war when the Republic Government of Rhim sided with the Pride Systems of Devoir Con. When he came of age, Troy quickly drafted himself to fight and become a Devoir infantry combatant; piloting a class A small inbound unit fighter. After just a few years of duty he volunteered as a D class unit fighter: The Devoir Resistance Fighter. To this day it is considered Devoir's most proud unit fighter. As a towering fighter it is heavily armored. They were mass manufactured on Rhim and shipped to other systems of Devoir at the beginning of the 20 year war.

As the demand for large unit fighter pilots rose, Troy became a known ace pilot. But soon his skills were put to their limit as the battle for Rhim raged.

Within his mind, like an old replaying movie reel, he watched the flood waters forming from the planet Rhim's Northern ice caps. Though most of Rhim's population evacuated on the planet's moons, Rheas and Ryleatu, when their government sided with Devoir, the devastation was over bearing. It changed the minds and hearts of people forever.

Inside his Devoir Resistance Fighter, Troy could only watch. The blackness of space all around him couldn't hide his words, "My God. How could we have let this happen?" The Nations of Earth laid waste to Rhim with new Experimental Nuclear Missiles known as Atlas Nukes or Super Nukes. "How could we allow ourselves to become this?" Arlington continued. Suddenly a faint voice could be heard. A woman's voice told through the violence, "This is Lieutenant Colonel Victoria Moore. I'm leading any and all Devoir fighters for a final push against those Earth dogs!" Troy was immediately snapped back into reality and answered, "This is Colonel Troy Arlington. It's a mess out here. Give me your waypoint to follow, Moore." A simple guide patched through on his HUD. Troy followed as the chaos of the battle also came into reality for Arlington.

Devoir Con forces suffered a heavy toll that day. All around him were the dying or the dead. Stray intense beam cannon tracers streaked across from large battle ship to battle ship. The shifting of dominance for the battle for Rhim was like two fighters holding each other with one hand while the other hand held knives. There was no cover to take in this fight or rules of engagement. Just a swift hand of the equalizer taking as it pleased.

Troy finally sees a group of seven Devoir Resistance Fighters closer to the planet Rhim. Only one pilot was leading the six others. It was her, Victoria Moore.

Arlington moved through their formation until he was side by side with Moore. "This is all you could gather?" said Troy. Victoria responds, "Only the brave need apply. We've been listening in on the Earth forces communications after their first strike on Rhim. Another attack is imminent on the Southern Pole." Another attack would completely ruin Rhim forever. Troy knew that the Nations of Earth had no right to pass such judgment.

"Do you know where it's going to come from?" asked Troy. Without hesitance she answered, "The main flag ship." It was just ahead of them; a behemoth of a ship. It moved out of its encircled fleet protection towards Rhim for an obvious second attack with armed Atlas Nukes. Its main guns aimed towards their advance. The beast fired once to test their mettle. The Resistance fighters scattered only briefly; forever moving forward.

As the brave came closer, the flag ship appeared sickly longer and out stretched than seen from a far with intricate designs and grooves on its outer paneling. It fired again; catching one of the brave off guard. Neither Victoria nor Troy thought twice to look back as one was lost in this horrific dance of men and machines. Ten glints could then be seen streaming about and around the flag ship. "Inbound Earth fighters spotted!" yelled Lieutenant Colonel Moore.

Victoria brought her twin energy cannons online. From behind her unit fighter they rotated over the shoulders; poised to fire when in range. She fired short bursts of exotic colored energy rounds that twinkled as they continued in the distance. All of the remaining Devoir Resistance Fighters found themselves in a heart pounding fray.

Round after round of short range laser fire came from the flag ship. Troy found himself personally side boosting away to avoid the beast's claws while firing his very large PX-3 rifle at the now merging Earth fighters. The Earth unit fighters are as large as their Resistance fighters but more brutish looking. Their weapons consisted of a right arm held Vulcan cannon, a large left arm held short range cannon and outer missile stores located on their waists. "Keep pushing!" ordered Moore. "That ship alone is our primary target!"

Troy Arlington watched Moore dance the dance of a fem destroyer. Through the thick of combat, Troy could almost see her face for the first time: Beautiful with soft eyes ever sodeadly as every rose does have its thorns. Her melody was to his curious growing heart. "Moore, look out!" yelled Arlington as an armored Earth unit fighter fired several missiles at her direct rear.

Moore quickly turns her fighter around while just missing the last missile by a hair of an inch. Troy destroys the foe with a single shot from his rifle. Victoria looks on at Troy. Finding herself in a smile, she wondered who this savior really is. "Come on!" she bellowed to everyone as she turned around while thrusting forward and onward. The other Resistance fighters gave excellent cover considering their dire situation. It was good enough to get Troy and Victoria in range of the flag ship.

**Large Inbound Unit Fighter: Devoir Resistance Fighter
Victoria Moore**

They locked on to the ship's bridge that stretched out boldly on top of its bow. They each fired their PX-3 rifles. It toppled under the ballistic pressure and sank within before exploding. Debris burned scantly while hugging onto escaping oxygen in the frozen blackness. Glass, beams, and paneling clanged and floated past their unit fighters. "That's it. It's over." said Victoria exhaustedly. The battle was drawn to an end but the war would continue.

As they watched the large ship float on at a high momentous velocity towards Rhim's atmosphere where it would burn then slumber forever, its still active guns fired aimlessly and everywhere as its crew screamed vengeance. But all too well victory has its price. And as Troy and Victoria found themselves together, a spark surged through their bodies that were undeniable and true. And as others perished all around and explosions triggered, Troy could only hear the slowly relaxing breathing of Victoria Moore.

Without their notice, the front end of the flagship burned as a large turret aimed its barrel in their direction with one final shot loaded. Victoria looked on at Troy with her unit fighter facing his. A rare sight to be seen. "Burn, baby," she said ever so softly, "burn." They both could only wonder who one another are within the chaos. And within their souls. The flag ship fired its final round as they were left only to wonder within their machines.

As Troy wakes from his more than long dream, he runs his hands along his aged and tired face. He brings his bare torso upright from the bed before pressing a small table light switch on that is adjacent to his large bed. The crampt room is lit just enough to see a very small window across the room, though small, the thick plated glass window shows bright stars illuminating half of the room. Troy looks on out the celestial bounty and gives an always strong inhale and exhale. He thinks the journey from Rhim's orbit to another system has been long.

Suddenly the sheets on the other side of the bed begin to crawl and shift. Getting up, Arlington tries not to wake the woman next to him who is still sound asleep. He walks on over to that which has always been familiar to him. Though the window gives a small eyeful of space, Troy remains as humble to the stars as when he was a child.

"Could you imagine where we've come from?" asked Troy to himself. "Could you imagine-" "Troy?" questioned the woman in the bed. She is fully awake in the dark while watching Arlington who doesn't turn away from the bright window. Sitting up fully in the bed now, she asks, "How long has it been, baby?" Troy responds, "To long, Victoria." She pulls the sheets aside from her black two piece wear and stands up. For a woman of her own age, she stretches her more than lean body while coming forth into the light. It has been sometime within the Systems Shuttle as it traveled from Rhim's orbital station all the way to the Chariot system.

They are under direct orders from the Pride Systems to meet a woman named Laura. All Troy and Victoria really know is that another war is at hand. Moore wraps her warm arms around Troy, hugging him close. She breaths him in ever so sweetly. But Troy has his own thoughts on this mission. "I hope this pilot, Laura, is worth it." said Troy bluntly. Victoria chuckles gently. Her soft eyes look on out the glass window; trying to catch what Troy is thinking. Troy is thinking about his love, Victoria, and her place with him in another war.

Troy knows that Victoria bears the scars of the 20 year war. When the flag ship fired its final cannon round during the battle for Rhim, she was hit and critically damaged. Moore's right eye was scarred. It would have been permanent if not for the technologies and advanced optical sciences of today's times.

She's tough as nails. An actual soft eyed tiger and Troy knows it. Victoria chose to continue to fight for Devoir alongside Troy as his second in command for a final mission that is the beginning of many missions for the end of youths to come. But Victoria was chosen by the Pride Systems personally to his disapproval. And it *is* their final mission;

he keeps reminding himself in keeping his beautiful long dark haired love in mind. Once it is accomplished he plans on surprising Victoria with another life.

"Mundane." said Troy out loud from thought. "Perfectly mundane . . ." "What are you thinking about, baby?" asked Victoria. Of course Troy couldn't spoil his surprised so he told a half truth, "Our mission, Victoria. No matter what, no feelings. 'Just routine as usual." "Understood." she said. "I'll stay alive one more day for you, Troy."

As they continue watching out of the small window, outside the deadly vacuum of space, there is no real war. They could only imagine what sins man has yet to create a new and soon. But there, where the field of battle has taken to the stars, is a presence that humbles all. Its remnants are evident in the planets, the stars, and the galaxies created. The pair lovers continue looking on like children that can feel they are home; safe and warm. And as they forever move forward they embrace the world of tomorrow that which is today.

MACHINE GODS OF THE ETERNAL SEA

CHAPTER 4

CHARIOT. A ONCE exploited world by the Nations of Earth sits comfortably nestled between its two moons appropriately named Chariot's First and Second Wheels. Chariot is mainly covered in vast oceans that which provides more rich and natural elements. Its two polar regions' size rivals that of Earth. But more interesting, Chariot is home to an aquatic race known as the Sentai. The Sentai were always a gracious race and participated in Chariot's engineering and growth as a highly evolved world. It was the Nations of Earth who set to re-educate the Sentai race. Under Chariot's Capital, Stage, before the civil war, Chariot was Earth's main interest in military stationing, aquatic ship building, and bases. Now Devoir sees it as a peace by ignorance.

Chariot is still a thriving world with a majority of its population in support of Devoir Con. The people of Chariot sympathized with the Pride Systems when the three Pride worlds declared their independence from the Mother World. As a world that emphasizes pride, Chariot withdrew its alignment with Earth and fought respectively during the 20 year war. Chariot has in fact been the best defended world against the Nations of Earth and therefor suffered no attacks on its soils or waters. This was partly because of the support of Chariot's specially designed Medium Inbound Unit Fighters also known as Chariot Warriors.

But at the end of the long and bloody civil war it was mostly all of the worlds of Devoir who had the worst outcome from environmental to economic disasters. Now this Earth-like world is ready to launch an ace pilot to set the path of war against the Mother World, Earth, once again. Though the future of Chariot seems limitless with the Capital, Stage, government conducting like one country below military officials and Devoir appointed magistrates, it was decided to follow this path of war to strengthen a weak hold by the Devoir Con Systems' worlds and become the conqueror of new systems and worlds under Earth. Chariot's ambitions are set to the closest of Earth held worlds for the future of the crumbling Devoir Con.

"Steady yourself, Laura. I guarantee you this will be no walk in the park."

"Understood, Commander Ward."

The desert floor swirls beneath Laura's Chariot Warrior. As Laura pilots it cautiously on the planet Chariot's desolate and barren equator, its gear movements are hushed by a constant howling wolf-like wind. Laura hasn't a clue what to expect from her Commanding Officer, Sarah Ward. It's unlike her mentor and former institute teacher to leave her in the dark about what she's up against.

As the honey sun shines down amid a very visible moon, the color of the Chariot Warrior shows off a bright blazing red that appears to set the desert on fire. Despite the awesome powers of her Warrior that Laura controls with ease, she is reminiscing on the times she and Sarah fought against Pirate Scavengers who smuggle military hardware for money and commit acts of terrorism against Devoir Con worlds. "It won't be long now." said Sarah Ward in a seat behind Laura. "You have permission to speak freely. In fact I primarily brought you here to talk to you openly."

"Ma'am?" Laura questioned while briefly gazing back at Sarah. Sarah was seen by Laura to have many thoughts just waiting to unlock and come out. Sarah Ward explains, "I've brought you here, Laura, because I understand that you've been personally selected by the leaders of our Pride Systems for a special operations assignment. I won't go into details of how I know this nor do I wish to understand your mission specifics. But I feel it is my final duty to teach you who you are. In fact you have always been my best student. Do you remember?" Indeed Laura does remember. Their common bond is in their perfectionist ways. And though Laura is barely pushing age 26, she has become an ace pilot; feared by criminals alike. And it was those lessons taught by Sarah when Laura was a child in a strict class room where she learned structure and discipline.

Then, Sarah had short, rust colored hair that grew fuller over the years. Laura maintains her admiration to the past by keeping her naturally blonde hair at head length. Laura is young and believes there isn't anything else to learn. Sarah knows she is confident but also too envious of her. "I remember. And I will not let you down." told Laura. Sarah nods her head respectfully.

Sarah looks away before explaining, "I've done and seen things, Laura, which neither I nor you could understand for Devoir under the Pride Systems. I didn't understand them. I just did them. And there are things that trouble me about you, Laura. You're good and the Pride Systems want to make it seem like obeying an order is just pulling a trigger miles away. Regardless of your mission it is the choices you will make that will determine if you will succeed or fail in life." Laura doesn't know what to say. For Laura it is as if Sarah Ward is trying to make an argument with Laura about the Pride Systems without revealing everything so as to not confuse her. Then what have they been doing for all these years? Who are the Pride Systems really? What could Laura say?

Medium Inbound Unit Fighter: Chariot Warrior
Laura Falls

"You've always been like a Mother to me . . ." dragged from the lips of Laura. "I don't understand. I thought you'd be proud. And what you're saying is-" "Blasphemous?" Sarah nearly giggled. "The Pride Systems do not make a God. And don't be fooled into believing that they can rent you as a God yourself." Laura remains silent. Sarah can only imagine what must be going through her mind. In fact Laura's face is blank and expressionless. Her thoughts are filled with missing keys to doors locked by time. Finally a thought crosses her mind, "Then who am I?"

Sarah, feeling more pleased that Laura is asking the right questions, responds, "Then it is time for you to learn who you are. Your file stated that when they found you on a confiscated Systems Shuttle that came from Tinota to Chariot you were just a baby with a tag on your wrist. Unfortunately, Laura, you were a complete unknown. The tag itself read of no Mother, Father, nor your own name. But there is one reference to a twin sister where you were found alongside on a war ravaged Tinota. When your shuttle did arrive to its destination it came to a very different Chariot that which sided with the Pride Systems. It was my squadron and I who confiscated the shuttle you were on; nearly wiping out everyone on board after their escape attempt failed. There was never any sign of your sister on board the shuttle. And for 18 years you, Laura Falls, have been placed and raised in the Falls institute where I have taught for many years. You were destined for civilian work during the first year of peace upon your graduation."

Laura continues for Sarah, "That is until I discovered who you really are. A pilot. I do understand that as my teacher you tried daunting me of whom you were and instead taught the importance of civility over war. I can only thank you for who I am today. You have shown me the important balance a fighter needs to be. I wouldn't have come this far as to be hand-picked by the Pride Systems after seven years of fighting beneath your wing."

Sarah shakes her head negatively. It seems as though Sarah's words were wasted. Just as she did try and steer Laura away from the lusts of war before she was 19 when she enlisted.

Frustratingly Sarah responds, "You don't understand, Laura. Why would the Pride Systems choose such a young pilot as you? You've always proved yourself to me so much so that you became a known ace pilot against Pirate Scavengers and criminal terrorists alike. Your life is just beginning. The Pride Systems could have chosen someone more experienced than you. Unfortunately I can't always protect you. But I can prepare you. This is why we are here today." Laura halts her Chariot Warrior. Through the sandy distance she is getting something faint and far on her HUD. "I got something." told

Laura Falls. "The on board camera is searching through all this desert sand in the wind. "Is this it, Ma'am? Is this also why we are here?" asked Laura. "Yes." Sarah said coldly. "I've arranged a live fire testing with another unit fighter. You'll be surprised to see who you're up against."

"Surprised?" responded Laura confidently. "No AI is a match for me." Sarah says, "Oh? I've personally tweaked this unit fighter from its core thinking to the functionality of its movements. You can say you'll be fighting against me. Now then, are you prepared?" Laura pauses before answering, "Yes." "Then it is time for the master to teach the student her final lesson." told Sarah respectively.

Something low to the ground moves fast; masked by the boiling temperature and swirling sands about the scene. But technology is on Laura's side. Finally she gets a positive identification on the unit fighter. "It's just a class B Unit Fighter." said Laura boldly to the sight of the four legged beast. "A Panther at that. Too easy."

With a mere flip of a switch, Laura Falls' Chariot Warrior shoulder missile siloes break apart and open. As she brings one armored leg in back to position herself just right she fires a succession of three missiles. Their bright plumes rival that of the sun. It wasn't long before the missiles' trajectory came up high then downward to the sands below. The three fiery explosions are wide spread. But are they effective?

Suddenly a single plume of fiery smog shot out high and streaks through the dispersing exhaust clouds of Laura's previously fired missiles. Laura reacts by moving forward to avoid the screeching, incoming projectile. Its war-head detonates just above ground for maximum destruction. As Laura continues to move forward, the sands behind her begin to settle every which way. She thinks to herself: *Interesting*.

Laura can see on her monitor that the Panther is galloping fast towards her. Knowing that eventually they will meet, Laura prepares to engage her thrusters at the right moment. It is a skill that the Panther lacks. Laura can see that the Panther isn't changing its position nor speed; giving her other options of how to attack. Though her Chariot Warrior is equipped with shoulder firing missiles she is also outfitted with a right arm shield and a left handed dual ballistic rifle.

In an instant, the desert pink camouflaged Panther continues on its war-path as Laura instinctively utilizes her thrusters up and onward; feeling the rush of power. Brashly spinning the torso of her unit fighter back around, Laura is met by a barrage of high concentrated laser fire from the desert floor below. Instead of firing a single shot, Laura finds herself dodging and jettisoning further up to get out of range of the Panther's skilled firing. She finds that the truth of the matter is that she has always fought alone and has survived in battles by her own wits. "Flying off will only end this match, Laura." explained Sarah. "You must destroy the Panther." But this time Laura wasn't alone in the cockpit. This time she has something to prove.

As she comes as far as her pride would let her, Laura brought her shield to her Warrior's chest which absorbs a few single rounds. With the Pride of Devoir behind her, Laura engages her forward thrust back down to Chariot's desolate dunes.

Laura fires her dual ballistic rifle down at the Panther. In turn the Panther stops firing to dodge the rounds which scatter the sands around. As the Chariot Warrior's automatic reverse thrust kicks in before hitting the desert floor, Laura actively looks about for the class B fighter. Turning her fighter mid-way around, Laura is met with a wide view of the now leaping Panther which brushes and scratches her Warrior. She finds her center of gravity off balanced which forces her to plant her shield into the gritty sand. But Laura remains one step ahead by replanting her Chariot Warrior's shield directly in front of her while giving a joust of her long double barreled rifle out towards her like an Olympian holding a spear. The metal gauntlet grip couldn't have been more firm on taking an assured shot. From within her cockpit, Laura gets the functioning auto aim confirmed in red and fires once. The shot is indirectly absorbed. Laura squints her eyes hungrily to the fact that it is still a hit. "Don't get too ahead of yourself, Laura." spoke Sarah while shaking her head. "Finish it." Laura fires another round. Though the Panther reacts coldly as if being pelted by the softest of blows; its armored face shatters to reveal black dripping fluids, gears, and workings within.

Surprisingly the beast begins another gallop towards her. As if unstoppable, the Panther's muscle-like gears tighten and give out a hard leap. Laura can sense that the droid beast is trying to get over her shield. She fires once more. The Panther's exposed under belly bursts open to unveil its entrails-like innards as it falls; dying out the AI core within and landing on the shield's edge.

Laura stands her victorious Chariot Warrior firm and tall. She gives the now useless Panther a good shove off where it plants itself hard into the sands low. Gusts of wind carries a golden mist of desert that partially consumes the droid's body. "Bravo, Laura." exclaimed Sarah Ward. "Then I guess you are worthy . . ." "I understand, Commander Ward." told Laura Falls. "As I've listened to you I'll try to trust my instincts more so in the future." Sarah follows up while watching her back seat monitor, "Good because it seems that your destiny is en route." They are both getting a very large blip on their monitors. In depth on their screens, it is something descending down form out of the atmosphere. It's a friendly Systems Shuttle that has traveled from the system Rhim. The very shuttle where Laura shall meet Troy Arlington and Victoria Moore.

Laura was given the instructions that Troy will be her Commander with Victoria being second in command. Laura and Sarah can see a visual now on the shuttle. Its bright luster and contrails show that it is headed for their artificial island base located North East of their position. Laura's mind now fills with the slight fears of the unknown. She didn't find too many of her missions in the past to be joyful. What most people don't understand is the down-times and an inescapable thought of never returning. But because of her decisions the path she has chosen remains set in forward motion. And because of Sarah, Laura understands that more than ever.

MACHINE GODS
OF THE
ETERNAL SEA

CHAPTER 5

It has been 129 years After Ascension and it feels longer for Jane Estochin within Devoir's dark holding cell. Her very long and rebellious blonde hair had nearly lost its sheen about the walls of her detention where above a very tiny window shows bright stars of hope. Hope that she looks up to every now and then with her green eyes. She moves her leg slightly about in her sitting position to keep herself from going numb. In doing so, her thick chained shackles make very little clinking noises.

"129 years, dad." Jane whispered to herself. "Can you believe it? 129 years since we really made things complicated for ourselves. Ascension: The day our Mother World inhabited the stars. I heard in some places they still celebrate."

Jane shivers a bit. She knows that her cell is purposely being kept frigid enough to feel uncomfortable. But she knows that her greatest enemy is the silence. Jane has lost all sense of time while losing count of the days she's been there. The "civility" of Devoir Con shows as she is kept fed regularly. Jane Estochin has trained for this as a former soldier. As she is all too familiar with the Pride Systems' acts during war and peace, Jane maintains her sanity by reminding herself to stay focused for her Father's sake.

But Jane feels more worried about her Father than her own self. And as if he is there beside her she begins the last genuine conversation she had with him before he too was taken captive, "There was something you wanted to tell me, dad? About me?" suddenly the cell room begins to darken momentarily; un-noticeable at first to Jane. For some reason she has been blacking out and having hallucinations in the process. That time she actually saw her Father, John Estochin. "It's happening again, dad." uttered Jane. "The food . . . It must have been the food . . ." Like a tree falling down, Jane lands on the cold floor. With her eyes rolling and darting back and forth to an inescapable dream, Jane begins to convulse slightly.

For Jane, the flashback she is witnessing now causes her mind to cling to the memory of her Father; an agreeable stimulus to the outcome of the moment in time. And to understand her and her plight is to understand the war on Tinota and a man named John Estochin who fought for its land, Tinota's future during peace as the Mother of Pirate Scavengers who plagues all the worlds of Devoir, and a betrayal in which Jane never looked back.

It was 27 days ago when Jane and her Father, John, were on a resupply run. As usual they headed out to steal ammunition, fuel cells, water, and food. John scouted ahead in an old rotor operated "bucket" of a chopper from the air just above tree top level. All the while Jane piloted the bipedal Large Inbound Unit Fighter known as the Rebel Panther. Though it is just a simple supply run, the Rebel Panther was fully equipped with shoulder fired rockets and an assault rifle. Jane moved moderately fast so as to not pass John whose functionality served primarily with recon detection equipment.

Jane's Rebel Panther was lightly armored and re-outfitted for high jump capabilities. Behind this unit fighter trailed twin large red flags that showed the battle scars of a hardened pilot. A pilot that was called the Scourge of Tinota.

Three of Tinota's five moons were visible under a dusk sky. Mountain ranges in the distance nestled about the forests; seeming unaffected by Tinota's heavier than the Earth's gravity. "We're almost there, Jane." Told John through his headset communicator. "ETA: 15 minutes." "Understood. Just keep lighting the way." said Jane.

They were still using old military jargons as they found it hard to break away from their past. John Estochin was once a Devoir Con pilot who found himself against Tinota and ultimately all of Devoir. During the war, Tinota was the worst nuclear struck world attacked by Devoir first who maintained a "crown" hold on all five moons. Each of Tinota's Artificial Bases was completely obliterated as Devoir finally occupied the large world.

But just as they left with forces directly from Earth on their heels, two of the moons, Polaris and Terrace, were then targeted. It was John and a few select other soldiers who were the last to witness, as ordered by the Pride Systems, that their abandoned bases remain active. Later, to John's horror, it was a proven conspiracy that when the Nations of Earth forces attacked with full nuclear assistance, an unconfirmed civilian death toll was later reported by a humiliated Nations of Earth. But that wasn't enough to stop Earth's advance on Tinota. Devoir continued a long resistance with the new aid of resources and facilities on Tinota. And as John fought he felt threatened by the Pride Systems for what he knew and at worse he truly was alone. He lived for that land and gave and took blood for Devoir.

John quit serving Devoir before the war's end. It was more than chance did he come across a young girl named Jane who, like many scattered and lost children, was filtered into a government established disciplinary school. It was John's heart that brought him to adopt Jane for any sense of normality and peace of mind. Not only did she gain his last name, Estochin, but was taught and introduced the old romantic era of war and peace with stories of John's past that molded Jane into adulthood.

Jane was 17 years old when the war was over. John raised her to be a headstrong and vibrant young woman. A year later Jane became a Panther pilot where she protected the weak and dying civilians of Tinota from Pirate Scavengers and thieves. This was a good thing for Jane until the colonists' oldest threat had risen. Tinota's aboriginal dwellers, which humanity now refer to as the Terrors, threaten all the lives of Tinota's colonists.

Tinota is dying and the Terrors know it. For their own survival in the fallout of the 20 year war, they have broken their "Human Non-Aggression Pact" that which was formed many years ago. Now according to the Devoir Con regulations: Those who aid or sympathize with the Terrors will be executed.

John felt strongly that Jane's "future stage" was unfortunate when she discovered that her Father became a mercenary who ultimately did work for the Terrors. Interestingly it was John's sympathy for the aboriginal beings of Tinota. Only God knows that his true feelings are for the well-being of his daughter, Jane.

But Jane chose to follow her Father's path. She betrayed her Panther squadron and the Devoir Con forces forever. Within time, Jane re-outfitted a very old unit fighter, painted it dark with striking red colors, and imbedded a double red ribbon insignia on its head just above the ruby red single eyed visor. From then on she dubbed it the Rebel Panther as a living proof to her and her Father's belief in true civility.

And as she razed a path for the Terrors and her mercenary Father, Jane had become known as the Scourge of Tinota. The Pride Systems took notice to her combat skills as the people of Tinota gave a mixture of awe and hatred.

"That's it. It's just ahead, Jane." told John. "I'm sending you a feed of the facility now." The facility is an old outpost located in a solid walled in area. It's very old and run-down with many buildings and hangars scattered about. John and Jane found the outpost just outside Tinota's last Capital, World Tinota, which was vaporized mysteriously after the 20 year war. This left their Parliament government collapsed; isolating civilians from each other. There is what establishes anarchy. A vast radioactive nothingness. And with all order crumbling, Tinota has been given by the Pride Systems, just a few months until it has bled out dry.

"This outpost has only a few grunts on its grounds." said Jane. "And there is no evidence of any unit fighters. Dad, I don't think we're going to get much out of this raid." John replied, "We'll take what we can. We're low on supplies as it is. It shouldn't be too hard to get in and out of this one, Jane. Our so called 'Terrors' are relying on us for what we can get." "I'll move on your go." told Jane. John said, "Your all clear, Jane. Just be careful." "I'm always careful, dad." explained Jane.

Jane moved her Rebel Panther fast towards the clearing. She didn't waste any time on scattering the soldiers on the grounds with her assault rifle fire. It seemed strange what little, if any, resistance they put up. Jane shattered the walled entrance with one round from her rifle. Debris was sent flying towards the soldiers who reacted by taking cover followed by a move back. There were neither electromagnetic weapons nor any anti unit fighter weapons waiting for them of any kind. In fact the soldiers just kept going back to filter themselves through the buildings of the outpost.

Never the less, the least resistance she encounters the better on her ammunition budget. In fact this outpost didn't even seem to be structurally prepared for an attack by a unit fighter of any kind. All Jane was concerned about at the time was completing her task. If Devoir truly gave up on Tinota, then it is up for the taking. High above circled John who felt comfortable enough to move in over the outpost. "Jane, there's something ahead of you I didn't pick up on." informed John. "It's an underground hangar!" Jane told. "Then that's where the good stuff's being stored. I'll go in for a closer look."

Large Inbound Unit Fighter: Rebel Panther
Jane Estochin

John didn't hesitate to tell, "Jane, wait. I'm not getting any chatter from the enemy forces on the ground. They've gone silent as if ordered to." Stubbornly Jane said, "So, what they're some sort of covert ops? Why would they leave themselves helpless against me?" "Somehow they knew we were coming!" yelled John. "Get out of there, Jane! It's a trap!"

A blinding light flashed before Jane's eyes. It was an explosion that rocked her deep in her seat. "Dad?!" yelled out Jane. All John could say was, "My God." From high above John could see that the underground hangar was completely dug out and destroyed. From the rubble and hellish sulfur ash and smog stood what appeared to be a large unit fighter. It had very large metallic looking wings that stretched and came down from its back. Its chest came down to a very slim waist with a set of angled and boxed in missile siloes on both sides of the chest. Its tint was of an anaconda green. But its mechanical eyes were of a striking blood red.

As the dust continued to settle, the behemoth brought its thick metal leg forward; pulverizing and crushing the gravel beneath itself. "Move, Jane, move!" yelled John in shock. From Jane's perspective, the beast spewed white hot flames. Jane was scorched; ruining her barrowed cooling unit. It fired again but after Jane was able to move back and away. "'Flamethrower, Jane!" John revealed in order to assist his daughter. "I'm on it." informed Jane while pushing her Rebel Panther even further back until she maneuvered behind a structure. She brought her systems fully activated including her jump capabilities online. Finally Jane popped opened her shoulder missile siloes for ready use.

With her Rebel Panther's back against the structure's wall, Jane heard the sound of a cannon that had never been heard by her before. Only the shaking in her brown and black sleeveless leather jacket could match the jolting intensity of the cannon's single shell smashing into the structure she took cover behind. "Jane!" screamed John in horror. He felt helpless as his only defenses were dual side mounted cannons; hardly enough to puncture a large unit fighter's armor. The structure crumbled on top and around the Rebel Panther. Jane wondered if this new fighter would fire another deafening round again.

She moved and poised her Rebel Panther's head at her attacker. It moved swiftly yet never too confidently forward but at a side strafe. It held a second weapon indeed. Jane's mind fluttered with her past military experience and know-how. The flamethrower, she recognized. But the other long and thick barreled weapon appeared to be some sort of Explosive Shell Super Cannon; more simplified than any gauntlet held cannon she has ever seen. And it stared down with another round loaded in the chamber. John couldn't stand it any longer. He banked down hard and felt as much of Tinota's gravity as he could withstand. He opened fired blatantly anywhere and everywhere at the winged foe.

The jade colossus's angled missile silo panels came apart and fell to the ground; revealing a vast payload of Long Range Stand-Off Missiles and Heat Seeking Missiles. In a brief moment it fired a single missile that tracked fast to the old rotor chopper. Its smoke trail curved and sped towards John's rear tail.

John instinctively yawed into the incoming missile while he released several flares. This was no time for Jane to get distracted. She fired several busts from her assault rifle. Though she scored a few good hits, she knew that this fight was going to be an all drawn out one on one battle.

"Jane, this thing must be experimental." said John. "We don't know anything about it so you'll have to get into the pilot's head." "Understood, dad." answered Jane. Jane swung her Rebel Panther out and further away from the ruined structure; trailing man sized rubble and debris from itself. The winged experimental unit fighter glared its head at the Rebellious Panther and fired another ear piercing round of cannon fire at Jane. The volley plunged and grabbed the ground deep in front of Jane. She knew that the reload of the cannon must have been a mere second. She was desperate in her seat to find any sense of comfort in knowing something about the experimental unit. Jane fired again; shaky and unsure short bursts. Jane found herself fighting to a losing chorus.

The experimental blinds the shot with hot and furious fire from its flamethrower. And it appeared to be getting closer. Jane activated her power cells to strafe and slide left and right on pure energy. And such technology on Tinota was "barrowed" of course. Any outsider could see that Jane was down but not out. She still had an ace up her sleeve. Or shoulder fired rockets, for that matter. She knew this fighter wouldn't see it coming. Confidently she dispatched her shoulder panels away. Jane's green eyes hadn't looked more ready in her life. The Scourge of Tinota popped off four straight firing rockets that shook her Panther's torso left from right; left and right again.

The noise of battle from the tumbling and washing flames and missiles released became eclipsed over an immense thundering crackle and blinding light that nearly swallowed Jane whole. As Jane brought her fingers away from her eyes, she began to piece together what happened. One or more of the missiles exploded short of its target. The detonation was due to the flamethrower. And though the target was not destroyed, that didn't stop Jane from leaving a smirk on her face. "Well, well." said Jane briefly. "That's game."

Jane slowly walked her unit fighter towards the experimental that knelt without its dual weapons. To Jane's pleasure, she saw amongst the blackened tint of ash above the anaconda green, sparks emanating all around. It was damaged. As an eerie silent wind had bat and swayed the Rebel Panther's long and flowing blood ribbons, it was John whose experience told better that the danger wasn't quite over.

"Jane, wait!" yelled John as his daughter aimed the Rebel Panther's assault rifle inches away from the experimental unit's head. " . . . Jane." Not only was it John's experience but his instincts that clicked in mind as well. He knew how she felt in the cockpit of a machine that gave will and took lives. He knew she was still human and afraid to lose her life and his in which, though small, was everything. During that time, both of their hearts had beat as one.

Suddenly, with one swift motion of the bruised experimental unit's arm, Jane's eyes were slightly blinded by what seemed like a red strobe light. Seeing that it was still active, Jane fired a single round. And like an old back firing exhaust pipe did her weapon sound like before it shot out and away from her gauntlet grip. With wide eyes, she saw that the strobe light was actually a hidden Gauntlet Lance which is a high powered focused-laser-blade that works surgically on armor. It had cut down her rifle's barrel. And as she pieced together what transpired, the experimental fighter's second arm lance streaked down and then crossed pierced her dark armored chest; just to the right of her Rebel's head. Warning lights began to flood in of a haul breach and critical alert. Once again it stood but with two secondary weapons gleaming red hot. It charged which gave no time for Jane to inspect and seal any chance of repair. It was close for Jane to nearly smell its ash from what she thought was a victory. They both use their power to stride as if on ice.

Jane was pushed even further back through the outpost. She knew she and her Father had to retreat from this fight. But the question remained: What was the other pilot waiting for? Jane thought the experimental was toying with her like she was a child. She had to get out of there. Jane engaged her jump capabilities on fast.

As she began her leap of faith she trailed raw energy from her armored ankles to the ground below. She angled herself just over the menacing unit fighter. Just as hope dawned upon Jane, the viper had leapt into a half spin that which severed the ankle of the Rebel Panther. Her now junked power briefly cut off and on before she felt a momentous CLANG and slide of gravel and dirt. Jane opened her eyes. There was a brief pause before she quaked to the screeching sound of her back haul being opened like a can. Finally her systems went completely off line. She was in the dark. "Jane! Jane!!" yelled John. There was no response.

He saw from above a large gathering of Devoir troops surrounding Jane's Rebel Panther that was face down on the ground. The experimental unit fighter uplifted its gauntlet lance from out of the Rebel Panther's back. John then saw many flashing lights spiraling towards him from the ground. The troops were firing on him with rockets; causing John to spin out of control and crash, as he was hit.

But who was the pilot of the experimental unit fighter? Who dared to defy the Scourge of Tinota and bring its rebel flag faced down? "Cero, mission accomplished." verified an official on Tinota under General Armada. "Your next task is to take the Iron Dragon and return back to your systems shuttle and travel back to Xiston. That is all."

As Jane was coming too from her worst case scenario, rather than nightmare, she finds herself being dragged away from the cold cell by two armed guards. Still a little dazed, the scene moved down a long hall of old degraded walls. Above were wide and thick glass panels that stretch and borders the dark and desolate outside. She can see alien mountains ranging as far as the eye can see. But more importantly she can see the large world Tinota; shining its bright blue oceans like the eye of a Goddess. She now knows she is on one of Tinota's moons.

They stop at an electronic door where one of Jane's escorts swipes a key card that opens the door like a slow moving vault. Dragging her feet ever further, a man stands at the end of this hall. Jane finds herself amongst holding cells. Row after row of cold steel bars lined left and right. "It would appear that the laced food we gave her this time was too much." said the man. "Can she stand?" Her captors shook their heads. With arms casually folded behind his back, the man nodded once. The guardsmen, in response, stood Jane up and threw her against the bars to her left.

With the toxicity of the drugged food still in her veins, Jane struggles to hang onto the bars. "Coward." hissed Jane. The man points out, "So you are alert, Jane Estochin." "More than you'll know, General Song." told Jane to the less than surprised man. Song is medium height with short dark hair, and is dressed stately in Devoir Con military officer attire. One of the captors motioned to strike down Jane until the General held out his hand to stop him.

"Say what you will but you both are here and only a select group of my loyal soldiers know it." said General Song confidently. "Both? What do you mean by both?" asked Jane dryly. General Song answers, "The other one put up quite a fight. We've gathered that he is important to you through the monitoring of your hallucinations." "He is my Father!!!" she screamed while lunging at the General with whatever once of stamina she has left in her. Jane was brought down quickly by both of his guards. She lies on the ground before the boots of Song.

The General nudges her with one of his shined boots to "encourage" Jane Estochin to look up at him. "It won't be that easy. Not even for someone like you, Jane." "Wha', what are you talking about?" coughed up Jane.

"You're good, Jane, and with your limited resources you've fought against your own and became a Terror sympathizer and mercenary. The Pride Systems have noticed." Song pointed out. As a former Devoir unit fighter pilot, Jane is familiar with the infamous General Song. But what could he want with Jane? Normally she would have been put to death for crimes against Tinota and ultimately all of Devoir; beyond Song's comprehension. Why keep her in an old and abandoned prison secretly? General Song couldn't keep them secret from her as ordered by the Pride. He continues, "The Pride Systems. Hmph. Their will, they have entrusted in me, shall be done. And that will, Estochin, is to once again raise the battle flag of war for Devoir."

Song kneels down to Jane. With a holstered pistol dangling from his outer thigh, the General never felt more confident in the loyalty of one of his disgraced former soldiers. This is explained by Song, "If you do not obey the Pride Systems' demand than you shall watch your Father die." And on that cold and rough floor, Jane Estochin knows she does not need to give an answer.

MACHINE GODS
OF THE
ETERNAL SEA

CHAPTER 6

T HE PLANET JUANTAN and its Earth like sun brightens and shimmers the red sands' top layer. Its three moons, seeming so untouched by man, have had their reasons to fear him in the past. Denizen and Bethlan are the moons that are more visible by the first of seven Capital colonial domes, known as Kontessa. Kontessa's shape resembles the Egyptian pyramids of old. And its veins, which Juantan's people travel through like blood that keeps the planet alive, spread visible about the planet's arid surface.

Though its civilians are at times hopeful and resilient on such a dead world with no oxygen, Juantan is one of the least wealthy worlds currently under the Devoir Con-Systems. But before the war, Juantan was once a strong mining and resources colony for Earth. It was the Pride Systems who ordered the destruction of most of its facilities; economical and otherwise.

Eventually the working class and even soldiers became abandoned like the resources they had coveted. It wasn't long when Juantan crawled with crime and poverty. The people were and still are uncertain of their future as an organized criminal pirate faction formed; plaguing Devoir.

But one could say that Juantan was always a dangerous planet with its unpredictable ionic storms followed with a deadly northern ice storm that swirls clouds of poisonous gases. The established Capital Colonies are the people of Juantan's only defense from the elements. It is an elaborate escape but not from the politics of Devoir.

All seven colonies are governed by seven Devoir Commanders who allow the people of Juantan to govern themselves with the promised freedoms of the Pride Systems. All under the watchful eye of Devoir of course. In turn the people of this world have upheld new ideas to raise the economy and attract tourism such as resorts for games and gambling.

Now Juantan is one of the most visited and diverse convoy traveled world and system. And as their industry slowly makes its way to the surface again, Juantan's three moons are now starting construction of Artificial Island Base and Defenses. An economic recovery has been seen by the Pride Systems as it is Devoir's hope that when another war begins, Juantan shall be a reliable world.

Darren
    Myzota

A man by the name of Darren Myzota awakens in a small, low rent, apartment room within Kontessa. From his sound sleep he finds a woman, his girlfriend, next to him. They haven't known each other for too long but she and Darren have found something in each other to keep an interest.

She thinks Myzota's personality is untamable. Darren Myzota believes she can find parts of herself in him. She tosses and turns a bit as Darren finds the sun's full honey light bathing them so richly. It is a rare sight for the planet Juantan with deadly gas clouds permissible. While looking out the room's large window with eyes as black as coal, Darren can see the rusty world, Juantan, more clearly. Its mountains are untamed and unforgiving unlike anything some have ever seen. But of course it has been a while since he has been out there as a pilot.

Darren casually walks past the alien view and towards the shower room. Shutting the door behind him wakes his girlfriend up who searches his side of the bed with weary eyes. "Darren?" she questioned to the sound of running water. She looks over to the shower room as a billow of steam clouds the cracks of the door. "I'll be right out, Sharon." told Darren. "Sure." said Sharon to herself low and condescending. "Take all the time you want." Sharon rolls her eyes. Of course she is a young thing when compared to Darren's untold age. But no one really notices how old Darren really is because of his youthful looking face.

Most of Darren's past is a mystery, even to Sharon, as he often keeps to himself. Darren saw the destruction and taking over of Juantan first hand as an arriving Devoir Con Tiger pilot. He was a short and scrappy pilot. Myzota was like a lot of young soldiers; anxious for combat and adventure. And over a short period of time he became an ace pilot. "Come on, Darren . . ." said Sharon impatiently. "I'm next in there and you know I have to leave soon."

One could say that after he and his Tiger squadron wiped out Juantan's defenses, Myzota had seen enough "ordered" conflict and grew old in his soul. And as a currently active pilot and soldier, he has seen the worst in others. Including him.

While Darren allows the shower to pelt and wash about him and drain below, in reality, it can never clean what he has done nor restore him from being a thirty something shell-of-a-man. Sharon speaks to herself while picking her nails, "What an outsider. He's just too . . . quiet. I share everything with him. But does he open up to me? No." Yet something snapped in Darren. His youthful attitude changed all the while getting into petty bar room fights. He doesn't back down nor retreat. Darren can only describe it as a thrill. A thrill and an excuse that led him down the path of a thief and Juantan Pirate.

It was after just a while of smaller offenses like illegally selling Devoir Con parts and equipment did Darren decided to participate in a pirate salvage operation against his own faction, Devoir. In a re-outfitted unit fighter, Darren slaughtered all of the Devoir forces that got in his way. The pirate faction of Juantan dubbed Darren Myzota as a ruthless hero. It wasn't long when his piracy made him into an unknown legend by the civilians of Juantan. But where this pirate ace lacked in respect, he gained fear by his fellow Devoir soldiers. And though Myzota believes he is safe within the shadows, he could care less of his merciless actions against the never blinking eye of Devoir.

Darren comes from out of the shower in just his boxers and approaches the built in wall drawer below the room's window. The warm sun, now less in full view because of the gaseous clouds, shadows then spot lights the room. As Darren pulls out the drawer to begin collecting his clothes, Sharon mocks by saying, "You took forever in there, you know. Oh, that's right. I forget that you do spend time on that mess you call hair." Darren says nothing. He just continues to fit on his loose wearing white pants.

"Aren't you going to tell me why you're in such a rush, Darren?" asked Sharon. Darren now combs his somewhat short hair in such a way that keeps it sticking up. "I'm heading out." Darren answered bluntly. "Yeah, I understand. But where? And would it kill you to tell me for how long?" asked Sharon. Unapologetically he responds, "'Don't know, Sharon. It's an assignment from my superiors." War and soldiers and the like are different to Sharon's "world."

From her perspective they are the instruments of death and destruction. It is a truth of one's mortality. Sharon may be brash and rude at times but she feels for those who fought in the last war. Especially for Darren who still has a job to do. But these feelings she keeps locked away to herself. It is a similar quality of Myzota that may have rubbed onto Sharon.

Darren fits about his red sleeveless over coat with the black leather patches on it. He then takes his black shoes and then walks on over to his side of the bed where he plants himself down. Sharon swivels her body across the bed to sit beside Darren. She gives a few quick and pouty glances at the dark haired and short statured man. Darren barely notices Sharon with her arms crossed in an uncomfortable fashion.

Sharon sits opposite of Darren's black tattoo on his right arm. And as Darren begins to put on his shoes, Sharon feels as though she should comfort him. It can only be described as a sixth sense as he is leaving out again. As well he can be a difficult man. He often hides his emotions like a scorpion's tail under his silent breath. She gives a long exhale.

Eventually her youthful wide eyes trail off to a corner in the room. Darren senses how exhausted Sharon seems. From under his over coat he hands over to her, in an awkward way, a large sum of Juantan currency. The stack of gold paper, that is banded together, widens Sharon's eyes to their full capacity.

Sharon has never considered herself a cheap date. But this was a considerable large amount of money and she wasn't planning to go all out on the town this morning. Though confused, she doesn't hesitate in taking the prize. "What is this, Darren? A war benefits savings? But-" pondered Sharon before being interrupted by Myzota. Darren says, "It's nothing, really. In case I don't return I'll leave this and all of my possessions to you. Is that all right?" Sharon nods her head. She is too smart to ask any questions from someone as quiet as Darren.

Sharon opens her arms wide and throws herself almost carelessly to Darren's torso; squeezing him hard. Surprised by her raw open feelings for him, Darren motions her away and holds her arms at bay. He then stares down, realizing he is only hiding his feelings from Sharon. Suddenly Darren Myzota moves his hands down along Sharon's arms until he feels his fingers finding her clenched fists. As Sharon slowly opens both of her palms, Myzota seizes an opportunity to kiss her softly.

The more than confused, youthful, and hopelessly beautiful Sharon uses her now relaxed hands about Darren's back; keeping him in place. A slight sandy tapping on the window can be heard throughout the room. And as it is ignored by the two lovers, who remain kissing, a sand storm begins brewing outside. Swirls of red sand slowly cakes and blankets the room's natural light. It is as if night has fallen upon Juantan again.

Darren doesn't care that he will be late for a shuttle launch. To him it is nothing more than an order by some superior who was probably instructed by a faceless Devoir Con dog down along the line. For Darren's concern, the mission he will participate in will not be the end but the start of a new beginning. Furthermore it is just a mysterious free ride through space paid by Devoir. It can wait.

Most of what he was told was that the shuttle will travel to a secret meeting. And from there he will meet four other pilots. But most interesting to Myzota is that he was told they are aces. Yet despite Darren's presumed loyalty and devotion to Devoir and the Pride Systems, he has chosen to make this his last mission and duty. No longer will he hide in the shadows for the crimes he has committed. He shall abandon everything and everyone he knows, including Sharon, to join the life of a pirate.

CHAPTER 7

THREE SYSTEM SHUTTLES align and travel through ancient debris that originated from a time when this unknown system was first traveled about. The shuttles are just exiting the century old field as the mangled chunks ahead become seen as small as baseballs in size. Against a blue sun, colors of bright red and purple that spans and swallows the blackness of space brings about the uninhabited world that the three system shuttles now find themselves in orbit with.

And just ahead lies a very old outpost; gray and barely lit. The outpost is large and partially ruined from a lack of maintenance. The shuttles dock side by side to each other without delay. The first to step foot through the outpost's docking walkway are Troy, Victoria, and Laura. Ahead of them they see a quiet running station. The personnel are few; scattered about the dull foreground. This is hardly the saturated image of Devoir; strong and iron willed. If they didn't know any better the outpost appears to be in a salvaging state of decommission.

Suddenly it is Jane Estochin who steps from the walkway just behind the three. Her eyes dart like a cautious wolf in a sheep's den. She called herself their enemy before. As well this place, unguarded as such with whatever treasures it may have, illuminates her thieving senses. Jane places her dark hood over her thick blonde head. It is as if she is hiding who she is or from what she used to be.

Darren Myzota finally comes forward and into the spectrum to break the silence, "Some party. And why and the hell have they chosen the middle of nowhere, for that matter?" "More importantly who has called us here?" questioned Victoria Moore. Troy Arlington catches himself staring at his love, Victoria, in wondering the same thing. Victoria, missing Troy's thoughts on her, physically points upward to a shadowy figure on an old constructed lift that's coming down to their level. Indeed this is a strange place in regards to having a lift that once transferred those on board the outpost from top to bottom floor; seeing that it is rusty and rickety now.

The figure can be seen while a spark from a lighter illuminates the scene. The five pilots see that it is a woman, unfamiliar to them, holding a cigarette to her face. She seems to be taking the five aces for who they are personally before exhaling her toxic cloud.

None of the pilots can say they are impressed while waiting for some kind of answer or statement. She casually leers down at the gritty floor while an announcement rings out over an intercom, "Pilots one through five have arrived. Initializing preparation of unit fighters." "There are actual fighters on this heap?" spat Darren harshly. The woman looks on at Darren coldly. Seeming to ignore his comment, she flicks her cigarette of ash with a devil may care attitude and says, "Well then, Darren, let's get started. My name is Lieutenant Kempt. Needless to say we know everything about you. All of you, in fact-"

"Files tell nothing of who we really are, Lieutenant." told Darren. Kempt takes in another puff before answering, "Good because here on out none of you have rank nor exist for that matter. Walk with me." Susan Kempt turns away swiftly and moves forward. As the five pilots follow, they are each left with countless questions. And yet each is determined to jump into the fatal fray of battle if it means achieving their ultimate goal.

As experienced and disciplined as Troy is, he couldn't help but ask, "Is it true that for Victoria and I this will be our final mission?" The Lieutenant answers as they round about a corner, "All will be coming back to you as promised. 'Everything for everyone.'"

Finally they come to a room labeled with scratches on it that says conference. Susan opens the door wide and properly folds her hands behind her while Troy leads the way in. The ever cautious Jane is last to enter; still wearing her hood. It appears that they are indeed inside an actual conference room; somewhat large and unorganized. It is hardly a place for a secret briefing on their next mission. And with an actual round table in the center of the room that is wide in its oval-like shape, file cabinets align both sides of the room's walls. Some of which are partially opened. Yet what appears to stand out is an older holographic projector that sleeps in dust heavier than what swirls about the pilots' faces.

"General Armada. These are the hand-picked combat aces you have requested." said Lieutenant Kempt loud and clear. "Good. Now shut the door." Spoke the General. Susan Kempt gives a hard salute as if she is trying to impress the pilots in the room. As well somewhere down along the line she has also ditched her cigarette.

While Armada, with an aging hawk like glare in his eyes, walks in the now closed scene with Kempt utters, "Ladies and gentlemen, welcome to Special Operations. From here on out you are ordered to keep silent on the briefing I am about to give." The General presents himself in a thickly padded officer's suit. It is Troy and Victoria who thinks it is strange that he would wear something meant for being in live combat on a ship so as to prevent bodily damage to one self when attacked. General Armada continues, "That means what is said here doesn't leave this room. Understood?" "Yes, General, sir." each pilot said. "Good. I understand that everyone must be weary from the long shuttle ride." Armada says while staring into the eyes of each of the pilots hungrily to get the briefing over and done with. "Please sit down."

The five take seats neat each other and quickly sit at the oval table. General Armada walks over and past the sitting pilots to the holographic projector. While he turns it on to warm it up, Armada ejects, "We are on short notice so I'll be as brief as possible." No one in the room can see the old man's eyes blazing green from the now projecting image in front of him. There is just a small glimpse of something round like a sphere peering quietly out from the side of his combat officer's suit.

General Armada continues while stepping aside to show the projector's full view, "Here is the Earth. The Mother World to some. And to many it is the cradle of our Universe. It sits as an untouchable marvel to those living on it and to any willing to die for it. Well the Pride and I say: No more. Lieutenant Kempt, show them. Susan walks over to the file cabinets on the left. As she opens the drawer the pilots could only wonder what the General could have in mind for them exactly. What they do know more so is that their combat skills are what is needed. Someone in the machine to pull the trigger.

She drops down on the desk a stack of pamphlets that are several pages thick. And as each pilot takes their pin-punctured papers they begin to look through. They read on the first few pages that there will be an Alpha and Bravo team and the use of Experimental Unit Fighters. All of which is under the bold and underlined words: Operation Trojan-1. Within the middle section of the pages they read the statistics of collateral damage, hostile activities and patrols, and operational success versus failure. But the one who seems more curious about the mission is Darren who quickly flips towards the end of the pamphlet where an unknown unit fighter's broken design layout lies in fresh printed ink. Excited, he utters, "I read that it will be Bravo team who will pilot the experimentals-" "Yes. You in fact will be called Bravo 5." interrupted Armada. "All of you have been assigned a covert number as Bravo team."

Troy is familiar with Special Forces operations as he himself was once in deep assignment for Devoir. He already had the privilege of knowing the Pride's intentions of starting another war. But he had no idea of the magnitude of which lies before him now. "General, with all due respect, I have more at stake in my future than what sounds like a suicide run." Told Troy. Susan Kempt looks on at the General surprised. In response, "General Armada calmly says, "All of your 'stakes' or situations you find yourselves in that brought you here will be guaranteed under Devoir's promise. All of you will get what you want and what is coming. And this *will* be you final mission."

That was all the aces needed to hear. To accomplish this sortie, for Troy, is for he and Victoria to live the rest of their lives away from war. Where ever the wind may blow. Armada continues, "The task at hand will be simple. All of you are to safe guard a 'Trojan' System Shuttle drone that will be carrying a stolen Atlas Nuke. Its target will be the Earth's northern polar region. While all of you are on board, the Trojan shuttle will bypass the Nations of Earths' Friend or Foe detection with a false distress beacon virus. After that you'll deploy as Bravo team from the Trojan drone while piloting our finest experimental unit fighters. Your primary objective will be to protect that shuttle at all costs as it slings past the moon's gravitational pull. Finally you'll have to fight your way to the moon's surface to escape on another shuttle piloted by Alpha team who will return you here. You are all dismissed." And just like that it was another mission. Told to be their final where each will get what they want. God willing.

As some time has passed after the General's briefing, Operation Trojan-1 is at hand. Troy finds himself staring into the ruby eyes of a behemoth. Its hardened head isn't as ridged as other unit fighters. Surprisingly it seems to have a spark of life within the almost flesh-like gears fused with its outer structural alloys. Through the plate glass, a ghostly reflection of Victoria's warm face peers over the side of Troy's shoulder. He doesn't notice until she hugs his chest with her arms tightly so. "So this is it?" asked Victoria Moore to the straight faced Troy. "Just another ride with you closer to oblivion." Troy says nothing as if he is trying to read what the experimental has in store for piloting it. Victoria smiles and says, "I'm sure one of these days I'll know what's in that head of yours." "I'm just . . . thinking." Answered Troy. "Don't you ever worry nor have a reason to fear?" "I do." She told bluntly. "I think of us."

Several feet away, Jane is also staring at the large X-Unit Fighter and thinking of her Father. The Experimental Unit has a broad armored chest; bold like a juggernaut. She touches the glass with her open palm; wide eyed in awe. Its thick chest is where the pilot's cockpit is housed. Jane takes her hand away from the cold plated glass and balls her fists deeply rough to the sight of the evidence that Devoir-Con has secretly massed the tools of death and destruction again. And to her Father . . . Jane fights back the tears while

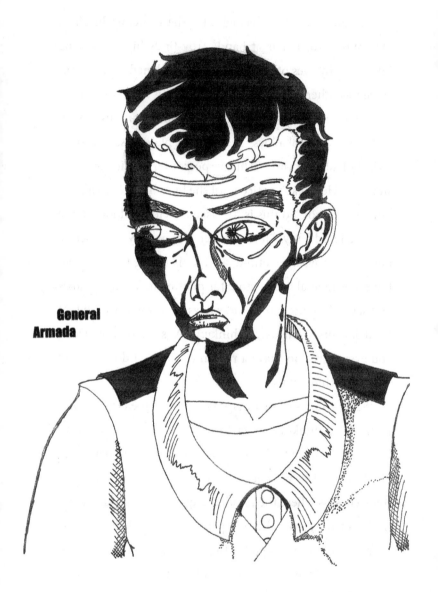

General
Armada

shuttering a bit. With John being held captive she has no choice but to be a pawn of the Pride Systems. "'Nothing to lose," said Laura, "yet everything to gain." Jane didn't hear Laura Falls step to the side of her. At ease with her hands behind her lower back like a good soldier, Laura takes in to admire the beast behind the glass. "I wouldn't know." Jane hushed. Laura points to the large and strikingly odd appendage to her right of the experimental and tells, "Look there. It is a hard-point appendage that can support its unique shield." Jane Estochin merely maintains that her hood is on in a cold brushing manner against Laura's spry. "And there," she points down to say, "it has gauntlets that support high intense lances." Laura couldn't help from smiling proudly. Jane is feeling physically ill and decides to wonder off for a bit of solace. "Hmph." Exhausted Laura who finally catches on to the stench of rudeness. She looks on again through the glass; missing her own reflection and more.

Jane Estochin rounds a corner where she stops. With arms folded, like she has an attitude, against her chest she leans against a wall. Looking onward she sees in the gray distance Darren Myzota who is staring down silently on a make-shift stoop. General Armada and Lieutenant Kempt are approaching him. Only God knows what the good General is saying to him. "Cigar?" Armada asked Darren. "I understand that they are bad for you but-" "Like this mission." Interrupted Myzota. The General hands him one of his premiere cigars straight from the fields of Chariot. Taking it, Darren puts it in his mouth as Susan swiftly finds a lighter from within her officer's jacket. He gets a good look at her longer than most men would dare to look.

He breaths in the fumes of the cigar and Susan Kempt softly; not caring or realizing how deadly each is. "You are a good man, Darren," ejected Armada, "unlike . . . some. Your file has been studied carefully by many of the Pride Systems as well as myself." "There's not much to tell. Just one man's career, is all." Told Darren Myzota who is still admiring the LT. Susan remains as unreadable as ever to Darren. "Exactly, my son. The eye of Devoir is always watching." Said the General as Darren quickly looks away from Kempt from the feel of his heart skipping a beat. He is far from being in love. Darren senses that Armada may know more than what he is telling. While placing his clammy palm on Myzota's shoulder, the General continues, "But don't worry. You will always be in my trust, Darren Myzota." Susan continues to stare at Myzota like a cat to its prey; knowing how helpless and human he is.

MACHINE GODS
OF THE
ETERNAL SEA

CHAPTER 8

IT HAS BEEN a long 48 hours as the five pilots adjust to the crampt living conditions of the Trojan System Shuttle drone. And as it is traveling through deep space on a direct path that is headed for the Earth's moon, the Trojan drone has been stripped of most of its interior comforts to outfit it with five Experimental Unit Fighters and its most precious cargo: An Atlas Nuclear Weapon. But it doesn't seem as though it is neither their mission ahead nor the fact that they have a pure weapon of mass destruction strapped to them that is bothering the pilots.

Troy walks past Darren and Laura who are sitting opposite of each other on modern red couches. Laura locks her innocent green eyes up at Troy. She wonders who he really is since he hasn't said much to anyone other than the second in command, Victoria Moore. Darren Myzota, on the other hand, appears to be more relaxed with both hands about the back of the couch.

Troy stops short of an electronic push-button door. As he gathers his thoughts and stomach which is filled with food that sits in him like a rock, he presses the enter button on the side. The door slides open to the left and there he sees Victoria who is once again staring out of a small window and out into the "endless black sea." Yet this time a somber reflection of serious thoughts can be seen by Arlington. Quietly he approaches like a killer on padded heels. While Victoria is still watching what can't be touched; her eyes dart from the corners of the glass panel. "Victoria." Troy spoke. She is still soft eyed to the eternal sea and lost in her thinking. But Troy is glad to have her alone. He is always pleased to have his love. A love he plans on keeping.

"You know I look because I feel something is out there perhaps watching us all." Victoria said to Troy in response. "Or at least should be there. Crazy, huh?" Troy catches what she is saying and comforts her. "No. When you're out here as long as we are you feel the presence of God. Not too many, like civilians, can feel this. In all that literal space you can sense that something should be there. What we do and who we are as soldiers brings us closer to seeing it." "Then I feel guilty." Said Victoria honestly. "What we've done and what we are going to do can't be forgiven." Troy responds, "Then we'll have to do this last one for ourselves." Victoria turns herself around swiftly enough for her dark hair to twirl about her face; shading a small smile.

A brief pause ensues before Troy says, "We've been through a lot, haven't we Victoria? Back before the 20 year war I thought I knew everything. And with a strong military upbringing I first began my interest in piloting unit fighters at a young age. That's when my Father was killed in action as a pilot against the Nations of Earth when the Republic Government of Rhim sided with the Pride Systems of Devoir-Con. When I came of age I brashly drafted myself to fight as an infantry combatant; piloting the smaller class-A unit fighters. After a few years of duty I eventually volunteered as a D-class pilot as the demand for those specific fighters rose. And then, during the Battle for Rhim, I met you."

Victoria hugs Troy closely and with melancholy in her voice she says, "I too was young once. Before that first Great War, when I was 18, I knew I would be a soldier for the Nations of Earth on Rhim's moon, Ryleatu. 'Just the same as anyone else in my family. But just before my graduation on Rhim's basic training carrier that was operated above Rhim's atmosphere, the civil war began. I was given a choice when my home lands rebelled: Fight as a soldier of Devoir or become a prisoner of war. They were actually willing to call us POW's. Their own people. It had not dawned on me the consequences of pursuing the betrayal of Earth. So I was stubborn and headstrong against Earth loyalists who were everywhere . . . And after all I have seen—"

Victoria takes a step back away from Troy. She turns around, touches and rubs her face in frustration then crosses her arms in self-doubt. Troy tells, "As you know I was given the opportunity to become a Special Forces soldier after we saved what was left of Rhim. I can't ask you enough to forgive me when I left you to go on deep assignment. It was my team and I who were the first to know the Pride Systems' intentions of starting another war with the Nations of Earth. On my first mission I led several other soldiers to Earth on an infiltration assignment in several defense facilities. Apart of our cover was being called Missing In Action until the day I would return to the safety of our war-torn world, Rhim. Victoria, I never stopped thinking about us. My sin is in not knowing what I had done. I paved the way for the possible annihilation of our original home world. I placed the fuses to the powder keg between worlds and the lives caught in between." Troy places his always steady palm on Victoria Moore's shoulder; rubbing it gently. "Then I guess we're in the same fire, babe." Victoria said. And then from the corner of her eye she sees in surprise that Troy is bending down on one leg to the floor. She turns around swiftly with eyes searching his feverishly. All that came out of Victoria was his name, "Troy . . ."

Perhaps it is the timing or fate. He looks on at Victoria without a proper ring. All he has is his will. Troy calls out her name in a warm and hushed tone, "Victoria." Victoria had already known the answer for quite some time. She forcefully nods her head within her still body and soul; not realizing she hasn't given him the answer he so deserves. And after nearly breaking down from her knees that are now weak, she finds herself lunging forward at Troy with open arms. While hugging him so strongly, she promises with a single tear rolling from her right eye she nearly lost many years ago, "I will never leave you."

Troy Arlington

And

Victoria Moore

Back in the main living area where no one is more the wiser to the weak hearts in the next room, Darren looks about in boredom and just catches the other pilot, Jane Estochin, in a dark corner. She has her hood down and is staring out a small window. Jane's long and rebellious golden locks seem to bring light to the darkness. "So tell me something, Darren is it?" spoke Laura. "What do you plan on gaining from this last excursion?" While still staring up at Jane, Darren Myzota answers bluntly, "Retirement."

Jane turns around in thinking that Darren is talking to her. Laura catches who Darren is looking at and says almost in a trance-like state to the more than familiar face of Jane, "For me personally, I guess there will be a war to fight." "And what type of war will that be?" Jane dictates. Darren interrupts and says, "Has anyone ever said how you two look alike?" Laura finds herself caught in her own words which inflame her mind to what Sarah Ward told her and says while shaking her head timidly, "My God." Jane continues hotly, "Who you serve will always be an ill master. And that master makes pawns of us all." Darren gives a loud Humph and smiles in agreeable ignorance.

Jane is visibly upset. Laura stands and as if to comfort her on approach, Jane gives a scowling look. Confused, Laura stops just short of Jane's wide comfort zone. "It's you. And after all this time . . . Can't you see me?" Laura confided with Jane. And Jane, for a brief moment, lets her guard down to look over the short honey-hair Laura. With the bits and pieces of hatred dissolving slowly within her, Jane is further able to see Laura through her cracked and broken mirroring eyes.

Laura continues, "I'm your sister." "What?! That's impossible! But you look . . . I mean our faces are exactly the same." told Jane who was in awe. "But are you the same?" questioned Darren plainly. "This mission and everything about it just doesn't seem right. You were the one who said something about being pawns. We were hand-picked by some General named Armada and none of us are without convictions. I don't like this. I don't like this at all."

But Laura and Jane weren't listening. For the first time what they see is just each other. "Come with me." said Laura. "What?" Jane questions. Laura continues, "After this sortie, come back with me to Chariot. There's so much I have to tell you. Much of which is about us and how we were separated." "Separated?" Jane questioned. And it was that sole word that brought her back to her thoughts on her Father. Jane, with her mental knives, cuts down her twin's heart with a simple reply, "No. I mean I can't. There is something I still have to do." Sadly Laura says, "Right. I understand. Of course there is something we all have to do."

MACHINE GODS
OF THE
ETERNAL SEA

CHAPTER 9

"ETA: Two minutes." said Victoria Moore. The five pilots of Devoir cannot see anything other than their illuminating cockpits that they are strapped into. The primary color of red shimmers like a beacon on their faces. Troy's breath catches up with him while his heart beats like the first time he laid his eyes on Victoria. Those were always precious moments in time he keeps to himself. It's very quiet now. The low humming of their on-board computers and interfaces catch up with the dead stillness; almost like being in a coffin as their sermon continues on.

"This is Bravo 1." said Troy Arlington. "Is everyone ready?" The hairs on the back of their necks stand on end and tingle. Perhaps from anticipation. Or the dead's warning from within the black celestial sea. Victoria answers, "This is

Bravo 2. Our weapons are intact and ready. I just hope this new shield holds."

A low unidentified voice begins to trail off unannounced, "We're reading your clearance now . . . Distress beacon is recognized . . ." Troy interrupts over the voice, "We're close." "My God, they really won't see it coming." said Victoria. Laura exclaims, "This is Bravo 3. I'm picking up a ton of hostile signatures. 'Looks like they are starting to encompass us." "It's nothing. It's just us moving towards them in this shuttle." reassured Troy.

The pilots within the Trojan shuttle continue listening to the chatter, "You have clearance to proceed. Welcome to the Earth System." Suddenly a light begins to flood their cockpits; pure and beautiful. It is the moon's glow that the five Devoir ace pilots can now see. Neither Jane nor Laura has ever personally seen the Earth's moon in person or even the Earth for that matter so up close. "Let's make this count." Laura said. Troy orders, "Everyone is to keep their personal chatter to a minimum." Darren interrupts with a low "shush" and asks, "Do you hear that?" Again the Devoir-Con pilots listen in on the Earth forces talking to the deaf Trojan shuttle, "There appears to be structural problems with your haul. Respond. This is lunar base facility 12 speaking, it appears that your side haul panels are breaking apart." With the Nations of Earth forces confused as to what is happening,

Troy gives the order, "Deploy now! We have to silence that base." The lunar base facility personnel continue, "That can't be right. I'm reading several heat sources emanating from within your shuttle. It's as if-"

The pilots step each of their un-named Experimental Unit Fighters out into the unforgiving beyond. With stars stretching about the scenic moon's edge, the Earth itself lies just in the System Shuttle's grasp and reach. "I have the target on our scanners. It's that lunar orbiting base further ahead of us stationed in the moon's orbit." informed Jane. Troy responds, "Than it's yours, Bravo 4."

Jane has her sights already lined up with the floating base. Though it is far from sight, she, like the rest of Bravo team, is equipped with double barreled high intensity weapons. Her smoother and narrower top barrel remains cool as she fires her rifle's bulging under barrel. As the glossy trail of fire beams and froths towards the orbiting base, Jane, as hungry as she is to accomplish her mission, didn't let go of her trigger as her cockpit fills with the hot glow of the weapon's discharge thus draining its power cells slowly.

The laser's final impact within the base and through its outer haul changes the color of the ends of the energized-sickling shaft. It is like flesh through a sword. As the base descends apart and rips in half, the pilots hear the maddening screams of those on board. It is enough to turn the stomachs of the most hardened soldier. But it is Jane who remains still as she thinks of her Father, John, and how he must yell out in torture every day for the return of his only daughter.

As the Trojan Systems Shuttle continues to move forward without a pilot's control of thought, the five pilots engage their forward thrusters located on the backs of their X-Units so as to match speeds with the Trojan ship for escort. "What are they doing?" Laura asked. Moving closer through the moon's orbit, the cluster of Earth ships within the vicinity have all gone silent. Contractual construction workers who are building ships and port bases, Earth security forces, to the usual traffic flow of a "healthy" world have turned their attentions to the now obliterated base. The elders who are witnessing this carnage are once again brought back to that long and bloody war. But it is the youths of Earth who will carry along the hatred for those who covet the flag of Devoir-Con.

"'Shock and awe. Let's use this to our advantage." Darren said bluntly. Victoria informs, "It looks like security forces are stepping into the ring." "Then they'll be our first wave." told Troy. "Let's show them why we're here." They each "paint" or lock onto a target from beyond visual range. The Earth security forces close in as swiftly as possible from all directions; unaware of who or what they are fighting.

And as security forces their jobs are to maintain peace and order above and around the Earth itself. They are the least of the hardened warriors of the Nations of Earth. Yet their armored C class unit fighters are light and well maneuverable for anyone to pilot. With their four uniquely long back appendages housing many forward thrusters, the security fighters' heads loom more towards their boxed in chests; giving out vulture-like glares.

One after the other the five Devoir pilots fire their long range high intensity beams at their targets. From a distance they can see bright explosions dying out quickly. And as more security forces close in, phased by their brethren's cries, an unannounced plea to anyone bellows out, "This is a distress call to any Earth forces who can hear this! We are under attack-" "Someone search where that is being broadcasted and shut them up!" yelled Troy. "There's an armored ship inbound for the moon." told Laura. "That has to be it."

It is a beast of a ship with formidable cannons and missile siloes about its bow. The small command bridge is at the very front end of the ever widening bodily frame. As the entire ace unit fighter pilots come under cannon fire by the inbound warship, they find it fortunate that the Trojan drone isn't catching any unwanted attention. In response they return fire. Round after bright and blaring round of beams streaks and illuminates the blackness. The armored ship takes many indirect flails but is still continuing now more so towards their formation. Jane points out hotly, "It's coming in fast! It'll try and take us out in one pass!" "I'm on it." said Victoria. Victoria accelerates onward towards the Earth warship at impressive speeds. Troy calls out to her, "Victoria, wait! We should stay in formation. You'll be on your own once the Earth security fighters merge with us!" Victoria responds, "Then there is very little time for discussion and I have only one chance at this."

Victoria continues her ascent onward towards the inbound ship. The warship's crews are all hardened veterans of the past Great War and chaos that surrounds them today. They have one single thought on who lies before their eyes: Death to those who stand in the shadows of the Nations of Earth. But Victoria is aware of this. She switches her left gauntlet lance on. The intense beam shutters unsheathed into the form of a pulsating blade that dies and narrows at the tip. As they gallop closer and closer to a point of impact, the small crew of the armored ship realizes the intentions of the approaching pilot who is carrying its hot glowing lance low and away.

The warship tries to brazenly dodge Victoria Moore's first strike by barreling low and slow to her off set angle. But it is too late. With calm, like the Earth's oceans deep, Victoria swiftly plants the beaming sabre deep into the "head of the fat snake." As she moves along towards the bow, she continually scythes the vessel. It is beautiful as the X-Unit Fighter's on-board Artificial Intelligence determines when it is time to let its prey rest.

And as Victoria turns her unit fighter around while cutting off her momentum stride, she can see the lifeless ship continuing its barreling descent towards her squad-mates' rear positioning. From a distance and where she stands, Victoria is witnessing the four others defending themselves with their shorter range barreled intense beam rifles against the Earth security fighters. Instinctively Victoria Moore switches back to her long range rifle and informs out loud, "This is Bravo 2. From where I'm at it looks as though the rest of you can use a hand." The warship's final play comes forth in which it silently brightens the scene as it shatters behind the four nimble Devoir unit fighters. Then like a boiling eruption it explodes out its outer shell and then twice from within its once living haul.

Troy Arlington utters, "Do your thing, Bravo 2. We'll take care of the ones in close range. You try to pick off the others advancing in on our position." "Understood." told Victoria. With Victoria firing bursts of pure energy from her weapon at anything approaching from beyond visual range, Troy, Laura, Jane, and Darren turn their tactics to short range attacks. They can see the enemy better now.

The earth security forces are primarily colored a spirited white to symbolize their righteous law. But it is their shorter medium range automatic weapons that test any judge, jury, and executioners' will. And they are swift to surround the four Devoir aces; separating them from the mobile Trojan Systems Shuttle.

"We'll take them here!" Darren Myzota encouraged loudly. Darren fires his rifle madly while diving into the mix of dodging Earth fighters. Surprisingly Jane throttles backwards from the group's formation with her unit fighter's armored arms open. As she spins around fluidly she catches a security fighter off guard and fires a single round through its lightly armored chest which kills its pilot inside. "Come on!" Troy told Laura. Just as that was said the rest of the surrounding Earth unit fighters merge and twine into the aces' formation.

The chaos that ensues can only be described as the highest point of a song that refuses to end. The beating drums of war continue as another security unit falls with a wound like a hole in an egg; spewing its inner fluids until it is crushed and silently illuminated in a brief explosion by the vacuum of their stage.

The Devoir Experimental Unit Fighters' gears move better and faster than its counter parts' like the edge of a sword swaying with the currents of water. Their fighters' functionalities are perfect in situations like these. These situations require swifter thinking to match their deadly weaponry. Suddenly Laura's left shield is hit which absorbs the multiple shells on impact. "Get away!" Laura screamed while cutting her attacker's unit fighter torso in half with her gauntlet lance. Behind her is Troy who is already engaging two foes. He quickly stabs the closest with his own beaming gauntlet lance and fires upon the other with his rifle. It is as if they are fighting against children. The battle is in Devoir's favor and the ace pilots will let nothing stop them from achieving their ultimate goals.

Just as suddenly as another security fighter becomes a victim to another deadly, rushing blast, a dark and brooding voice calls out from within the menacing and vast black sea, "We have clearance to use deadly force. Do what is necessary to stop this madness." Troy Arlington notifies, "I'm picking up more chatter from the Earth forces. There is something else out here . . ." "Check your interfaces and screens. We have more hostile signatures approaching." Victoria said. "I see them. They're large fighters moving twice as fast as the security units." Jane Estochin informed. They are coming from the moon's surface; showing up as small shining glints from a distance. They represent themselves as the menacing, winged fliers of the Nations of Earth. And they are coming to join the fight against the Devoir-Con aces.

Their formations, as seen, are perfect though they are bulkier and more heavily armored with old and hammering-idealistic-world weapons. But it is their pilots within the machines who cannot be bought nor sold to another flag. These hardened warriors of armor carry the scars of the 20 year war and other more recent conflicts that try the will of Earth. The battle is truly just beginning. These uncanny fighters under the Nations of Earth shall clash brutally under their sole world's ideals. As for the five Devoir pilots, their fates through the upcoming fierce battle will be tested as the message to the Earth as a whole will either be swift or slow.

MACHINE GODS
OF THE
ETERNAL SEA

CHAPTER 10

"We have inbounded Copper Heads closing in fast!" Darren Myzota called out loudly. The Copper Heads, flying twice as fast as the Earth security forces, are now in firing range of Troy and his three other pilots, Laura, Jane, and Darren. Victoria is still significantly at a distance from the rest of her squadron.

The Copper Heads, code named by the Pride Systems, are equipped with built in jammers that make it hard for a target lock-on from a far. Without saying a word to Troy or the rest of the Devoir fighters, Victoria acts fast by moving forward to join the fight up close. The Copper Heads open fire with their heavy hand-held cannons. The shelling is intense as the volleying rounds cross and tangle through the already fighting X-Units; coming just hairs from their targets.

The brooding Commander of the Copper Head fighters of Earth orders his squadron, "I want our nubile underlings to hold their positions and remain here to pick off those fighters from our backs. The rest of you, follow me in close range combat. Let's show these terrorists 'Earth's pride.'" As the mysterious Earth combatant leads six out of nine of his Copper Heads into the fray, he couldn't help but wonder who he really is up against. Terrorism against the Nations of Earth forces isn't anything new. And acts of piracy are a daily struggle. But as seen by the Copper Head Unit Fighters they are fighting a less than cowardly enemy that is anchoring the fight over the Earth's moon itself. The Copper Head leader will question who he is up against.

"That one looks like it's going to be a problem." Told the Copper Head leader who is keeping a situational awareness to Victoria's closing presence. And with that said, one of the Copper Heads behind the Earth lead fighter announces, "I have this one, Commander Tenam." "Roger that. Make it clean." told Tenam. The obedient Copper Head peels high and dashes in long bursts towards Victoria while trying to avoid the primary fight at hand. "Victoria, there's a snake in the grass headed towards you!" Troy informed desperately.

Troy brings his attention to the fast Copper Head. To his surprise it is evading every which way against Troy's onslaught. From left to right it evades his rifle's firing until Arlington is physically pushed by the hulking armor of Commander Tenam himself. "That's it!" said Tenam enthusiastically. "That's the way I like it!" Tenam aims his cannon directly at Troy's Experimental Unit Fighter's head. Troy brashly dashes forward at the Earth Commander to briefly confuse the advisory's tracking capabilities. The reaction sends both fighters twirling in opposite directions. But it is Troy who swirls his bipedal war machine around first before Tenam could. The Copper Head Commander sees this and strides about in a circumference as Troy fires his weapon in frustration. "Troy!" Victoria called out in a panic. "Hold on, Bravo 2," told Troy Arlington, "I'll be there to assist." As Troy disengages Tenam and soars towards Victoria, Commander Tenam picked up on their chatter.

Tenam simply flips a switch within his cockpit that makes his dual shoulder missile panels come apart and float off; exposing six large missiles waiting inside. Tenam says while firing off two missiles, "Terrorist dog!" "Troy, watch out!" informed Victoria. Arlington spins around and in the chaotic scene of witnessing death at an edge within this black realm, time seems to slow enough for the Devoir pilot to adjust his shield to take the utmost damage. And just as he is ready, the first projectile whirls past him which explodes short of his armored back. As for the other, its direct impact on the experimental shield causes it to ripple and quake as the massive explosion expands as far as possible; brightening every fighter who dared to see. Tenam grits his teeth and gives a low growl like a beast in Earth's jungles. He then dashes straight for Troy.

Interesting enough, Commander Tenam has his main weapon held down and away. Could it be that the Earth Commander is searching for another option to take down his foe? If Troy was paying attention to his main concern behind him, he should realize that Tenam has a more powerful lance attached to his unit fighter's left arm. "I'm coming, Victoria!" yelled Troy. What Troy is witnessing is Victoria's fighter struggling desperately to survive against one of Tenam's Copper Heads.

Troy fires s burst of raw energy at Victoria's advisory. From his distance he manages an indirect hit on the Copper Head's back; briefly stunning and catching the unit fighter by surprise. It is just enough for Victoria to stab the veteran pilot through its armored chest. As it falls away while trailing clouds of gases and vapors, the lifeless Copper Head bursts in an explosion from its fatal wound.

Tenam finally catches up with Troy's mysterious X-Unit. He gives out a hard lash with the twist of his torso. The energizing, pulsating blade appears longer and more deadly than the Devoir aces'. Only by a hair does the lance miss Arlington. Tenam swipes away and then brings it back again. The old Brit. Commander is well adjusted in a unit fighter fight.

Victoria Moore hauls her engines forward at full throttle to assist Troy. And with Tenam's jammer still active she knows that she will have to get in good range. Unaware of Victoria's help, Troy strides backwards on his thrusters just far enough to activate his own gauntlet lance. A pause commences before Commander Tenam says, "Alright then. Come on!" Troy then pushes forward and like a thief in the night, his prize is the charismatic Earth Commander. Just seconds before Troy's lance can slash his enemy, Tenam is able to block the force of the blow with his more than sickle-like energy blade.

They lock eyes on each other's unique unit fighters with eyes in hate. It seems like an eternity until Commander Tenam opens up with, "I don't know what you terrorists have to gain here but I won't allow this madness to continue." Troy disengages his forward thrust and backs away slowly and says, "Terrorists? Look around you. This is a declaration of war." Confused, Tenam says, "This is Commander Nathaniel Tenam of Earth. You are all in violation of Earth law. Surrender now."

Suddenly Darren Myzota can be heard laughing to his self before saying, "Can you believe this guy? Is he deaf?!" Troy can feel his breathing calming again. Commander Tenam ejects out loud, "How dare you. Unless of course . . . No, that can't be. We've had 9 years of peace. How could you? How Could You?!"

Tenam's Copper Head weapons arm raises, pointing his large cannon at Troy's X-Unit. He didn't hesitate to fire round after round aimlessly. In an almost hushed and slow piano wire balance did Troy manage to dodge every fiery blow. Victoria gives out a painful sound deep from within her belly. "What?! Victoria!!!" Troy wailed. "You butcher!" Victoria was hit beside Troy as she just arrived. One of Tenam's single rounds ripped away most of her entire armored right arm that was holding her weapon. "Hmph. Then you're all no better than mercenaries." Nathaniel Tenam dared to speak. "Die as the same!"

Tenam boosts forward at Troy and lunges at him with his long and beaming arm sabre. Enraged at the thought of Tenam's attack that damaged his love, Victoria, Troy fires a single shot at the Commander with his beam rifle. The hit to his unit's right chest causes Tenam to jerk and smack his dashboard interface from within his cockpit. A scar and blood runs across his face. Troy fires again. Tenam quickly catches his second wind and backs away to avoid the burst.

"This is far from over." spat Commander Tenam. "Requesting assistance from all pilots to merge with these Devoir fighters to take them out!" "Victoria, are you alright?" asked Troy. Victoria responds, "I've sustained heavy damage but this fight is getting out of hand."

"What's this?!" questioned Laura Falls loudly. "There's something targeting us from the moon's surface." Jane yells out, "Incoming missiles! I'm reading a single source that they are coming from." Just as that was said, the source bursts at fantastic speeds towards the ongoing fire-fight between Earth and Devoir-Con forces.

"Incoming!!!" Darren yelled as a long range energy weapon shot through the melee. But something is different about this beam weapon. Instead of trailing off it remains in a stable field of flux and flow until . . ."Watch out!" Tenam told one of his Copper Head fighters. The blinding beam moves through the blackness of space in pursuit to cut down the large unit fighter like a fly. For a moment the fighting seems to have ceased as everyone is caught in surprise and awe. The continuous laser beam moves again to find another victim. It finds another Copper Head who fleas helplessly yet futilely. And just as suddenly as it appeared it was gone.

"We still have incoming missiles to deal with." told Victoria who is "limping" her X-Unit closer to Troy's. "Don't worry, Victoria. We'll get through this somehow. I promise."

Troy said. Victoria catches her, breath and responds, "Don't talk like that, babe. I'm not through yet."

The missiles, though few in numbers, suddenly appear to be splitting apart and multiplying. As many of them now hurdle in a cloud-like formation of twinkling star-like projectiles towards the Devoir aces and Earth fighters, Troy orders his squad, "Open fire on those missiles. May be we can reduce some of those incoming numbers."

Troy guards Victoria by placing his X-Unit in front of hers while firing volleys of his long range beam rifle. They are able to bring down a few but the remaining keep coming. "What are we dealing with, Troy?" asked Victoria as Arlington kept firing. Troy responds, "They're some kind of 'spread missiles' yet I've never seen anything where one becomes three." "Brace yourselves, men!" yelled Commander Tenam. The missiles search for their targets in more than pairs of two as they come in full view to all of the pilots above the moon. Darren side steps one of the tracking projectiles. He watches its bulbous warhead sling its frail body about his unit's armored chest and dash towards a Copper Head fighter. The explosion decimates the unit fighter like another second sun that fades within the dark and scattering debris.

Darren can see two more missiles headed his way. He fires on one with his rifle, causing a bright explosion. The other missile reacts by giving a half loop around the dying missile's burst. "They're heat seekers!" informed Darren. "Which means what?!" asked Jane in frustration. Darren answers, "We can fool these things just by taking one out.

While several missiles approach Troy, he tells Victoria, "I won't leave you behind." "I know." Victoria responded. "I know." Troy fires on two that causes a dual eruption. Two missiles follow out from the cloud of shrapnel and debris and bank away from Troy and Victoria. Troy's grip on his fighter's controls loosens as he finds himself calm again. Beads of sweat begin to cool his brow while Commander Tenam, who remains in front of him, stands in disbelief of what is happening. His squadron is nearly wiped out by this unknown attacker's missile barrage. And as for the mysterious: It is none other than the infamous child soldier, Unit 0.

Now code named Cero, he is piloting the Large Inbound Experimental Unit Fighter known as the Devil's Son. Both Cero and his fighter are madness-born from the hands of diluted men. And to rage a war of men for the better of a future? Perhaps. But to destroy a 14 year old boy's life in a sick idealist's agenda? Then perhaps there is no greater sin than murder itself.

"It's here." hushed Darren to himself. Darren begins to power to the red unit fighter. "Wait!" called out Lauren to Darren. "Just like us this fighter is new and clearly not manufactured by the Nations of Earth." "That makes very little difference to me." said Darren. "I'll cut him down like all the others!"

Darren fires a single round at the Devil's Son. Its pilot, Cero, activates its shields which produces a thin and transparent veil across and around the red body of the unit fighter. Darren is shocked to see that his laser beam round has become within the veil. "What are you?" asked Darren out loud. Each pilot, including Commander Tenam, is witnessing something that is not of the hands that made them. The Devil's Son is a new weapon of man. A weapon whose barrel they now find themselves helplessly within. And its sole pilot, Cero, will be their judge. The one who will place their fates in the proper places.

But surprisingly Cero backs away and begins to head towards the ever speeding Systems Shuttle. Victoria manages to cough up, "It's headed for the shuttle . . ." Just as suddenly as that was said, Laura, Jane, and Darren race towards the Devil's Son. A panic stricken Jane blurts out, "We'll have to get in close to take it down!" The blank and expressionless Cero catches the chatter by Jane and turns his fighter about on a dime.

And while still on good momentum for the Trojan shuttle, he raises his left arm weapon which safely cuts through the energizing veil. Unlike his right arm rifle, this is indeed a cannon. Though it is unlike anything they have seen before, this monstrosity against nature must have been the one that cut through Tenam's men from a far. Such a blatant move appears desperate.

He isn't desperate. Cero is sure of himself. "Move. Move!!!" yelled Darren who moves back and then away; nearly knocking into Jane's unit fighter. Each of the pursuing Devoir aces scurry from this dominate player in this battlefield-stage. But would he fire? Cero couldn't have pushed the trigger more calmly than any regular soldier.

The sudden "wash" of energy blinds everyone as a stream line of a laser-burst can be seen for miles on end. In the silent void echoes through what everyone is witnessing until Victoria shrieks through the silence, "Troy!!!" Arlington was hit. The light was so bright that no one, including Troy, knew that he was going to take damage. How and to what extent? Troy's weapon is nearly blackened, melted and welded to his gauntlet while his armor is charred beyond repair.

"Troy?" questioned Victoria. It is a miracle that he still remains. Troy doesn't respond. It is truly a miracle that Cero didn't finish what he started. The young boy is given enough time to reach the Trojan Systems Shuttle. The sisters, Laura and Jane, watch as their ultimate rival boards the large shuttle. Darren feverishly flies to join up with Victoria who is emotionally chasing ripped pieces of herself that are blowing in the wind. Their mission isn't over yet and Darren is the first to realize this.

"Come on. Snap out of it, Bravo 2!" told Myzota assertively to Victoria Moore. "No! I, I can't just leave him! 'Leave him like this . . .'" Victoria drifted while sobbing. "'Fine, then I'll drift him to the moon's surface." told Darren. "We'll have to hurry in order to meet Alpha team while the Earth Forces here are dumbfounded." Victoria says while gathering herself, "Right, then. Bravo 3 and 4, cover us. We're getting the hell out of here."

As the Devoir aces begin to take a flight path to the moon's surface, the Trojan ship now banks off course from the Earth and away from its moon. It then engages maximum speed; disappearing into deep space. Victoria says honestly, "Troy, I don't know if you can hear me but we're almost home."

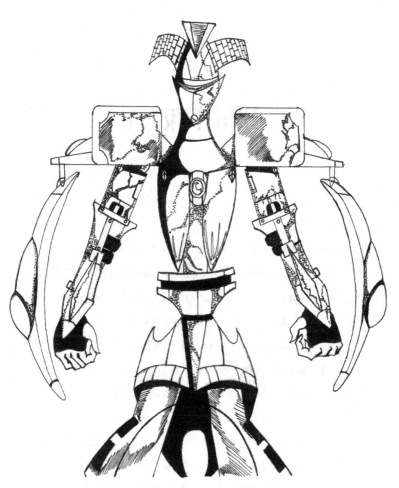

Large Inbound Experimental (X) Unit: Devil's Son

MACHINE GODS OF THE ETERNAL SEA

CHAPTER 11

EVER SO CALM and gentle does Darren Myzota align his experimental shield up against Troy's charred X-Unit. "Come on, Bravo 1," told Darren respectfully, "we're getting out of here." Darren then engages his forward thrust for the moon's surface. Victoria, still shaken by the strike on her own unit by Commander Tenam, follows close behind Darren. Further ahead is Laura Falls who gives the heads up, "Looks like Alpha team is stationed in plain view. They're nestled between civilian structures." Darren replies, "That's perfect. I'm not reading any Earth defenses there. We should be able to walk right in." "Not before the Copper Heads have a say." interrupted Jane Estochin. "Here they come." Darren barks, "Everyone, maintain formation. Our focus is to escape together."

"We're not finished here!" said Nathaniel Tenam boldly. "Take them out with extreme prejudice!" The Copper Heads dash without hesitance towards the Devoir ace pilots. "That's it." Victoria said. "Everyone, open fire!" Darren aims his laser weapon upon the closest foe and says, "You heard the lady!"

He fires a single round that crosses past Jane's discharge that gives them both a deadly hit. Their target's armored torso is silently snapped backwards with vaporous clouds following suit before the expected explosion. Commander Tenam, who is ahead of the pack, doesn't look back at the destruction of his own which was caused by the two Devoir aces. While galloping and pushing himself further and further towards the path of brazen insanity, the Earth Commander once again has his main weapon down low. "Prepare for close range combat!" shouted Laura Falls. Darren says out loud, "Again, huh? This guy is mine!" "No. We'll need you more than ever, Darren." Victoria spoke. "Troy and I are . . . Don't worry about us. I'll carry him to the Earth's moon. Just keep us covered."

And just as that was said, Commander Tenam orders bluntly, "Cover me. Their 'King' is down and their 'Queen' is completely vulnerable. She's mine."

Victoria gives a hard push behind Troy's crippled X-Unit Fighter and continues to head closer to the Moon's surface.

Tenam's squadron peels off towards Jane, Laura, and Darren while the Earth Commander ignites his deadly arm sabre. Darren, who has never taken his eyes off of the approaching Copper Heads, fires blatantly in an attempt to confuse and disorientate the metallic fighters. As they swarm about Darren's position, the cocky Myzota activates his gauntlet lance and slashes through an enemy fighter.

Jane and Laura fully support Victoria's descent to the moon; firing at Tenam's vexing units before they could strike. All the while Commander Tenam over-shoots Myzota's aimless firing. In realizing that Tenam has a blood lust for Victoria and Troy, Darren spins about smoothly to open fire on the deadly Copper Head. The intense beam tracers miss Tenam. Darren can plainly see the large sabre emanating from Tenam's left armored arm. He fires up his forward thrusters to catch Tenam with a better shot from behind. Nathaniel Tenam suddenly hauls his thrusters further away from Victoria and Troy which follows a long bank back towards Darren.

Darren realizes that the Earth Commander has him in his sights before he can strike down Victoria and Troy. In a bold move, Darren kick starts his forward thrusters with his right arm weapon held low. Tenam senses the Devoir pilot's intensions and calls his bluff by increasing his velocity towards Darren with his arm sabre still active. The dueling combatants finally reach each other. Tenam wastes no time in giving a harsh slash for the head of Darren's X-Unit as Darren unleashed his gauntlet's intensive beam.

The silent strike became quickly evident that it was Darren with the successful hit that pierced Tenam's chest armor. And with gasses escaping and fading into space, Nathaniel Tenam ignores the damage and fires a round from his cannon at Myzota. But as Darren continues to engage at close range towards the frustrated Earth Commander, Tenam acknowledges, "Something isn't right . . . These are no ordinary fighters."

With Tenam distracted, Victoria guides Troy to where Alpha team is signaling. "There it is, Troy. The Systems Shuttle is just ahead of us." Victoria said to a silent Troy. The very large ship lies up right for onward travel away from the moon's surface. Surprisingly it *is* in plain sight amongst civilian structures.

Victoria and Troy's landing on the moon's surface is relatively smooth. They are met by Jane who moves ahead to make sure they have a clear path towards the waiting Systems Shuttle. Laura hovers just above them while laying cover fire against the inbound Copper Heads. The Copper Heads open fire in response. Victoria, along with Troy's crippled unit fighter, are nearly hit as the Copper Heads' cannon fire strafes the moon's surface; causing pockets of pluming craters about them to form. Darren realizes he is needed on the moon's surface. He discharges one more intense beam at Tenam who roughly dodges before he kick starts his propulsion further towards the Earth's moon.

As he comes into good range with the Copper Heads who are continuing their assault on the rest of Bravo team, Darren grits his teeth and with the spirit of vengeance within himself he open fires. He fatally wounds two enemy unit fighters. Their fall from grace is almost as opposite as Darren Myzota's rugged landing on the moon with the rest of his squad. "Come on. We're moving now!" Victoria ordered. "Use these civilian structures as cover." Victoria can see the shuttle just up ahead in its own clearing. She can't move as fast as the others with Troy's unit fighter in tow. All she can do is pray.

The remaining Copper Heads are hesitant to use full force around the civilian populated structures. Commander Tenam senses this. He now realizes their scheme. And it is obvious to him where they are headed. Pushing himself at full burn towards the moon, the Earth Commander weighs in his choices on how to approach the situation. Tenam orders, "All who remain in my squad: Cover me. It's time to end this!"

The Devoir aces are starting to clear the civilian housed populace. Laura is first to propel forward with fear mixed in with adrenaline. All of their hearts are pounding incessantly as Darren engages his forward thrusters before Jane matches speed with Laura. Just before Victoria attempts to do the same, she adjusts her balance and hold on Troy. She knows she'll have to drag his X-Unit's armored legs across the gray "field" while not realizing who is bearing down on her.

It feels like the longest dash for the waiting Systems Shuttle. Instinctively Darren twists his unit fighter's torso enough to see, with his onboard visual sight, Victoria who is just making it onto the wide open field of gray. Yet strangely enough the Copper Head fighters remain poised above the civilian structures and colony housings.

"Something's wrong." told Darren. As Darren comes to a complete halt in his tracks, he can see past Victoria's sluggish progression. And what is there, amongst the habitable civilian colonies, comes at a high rate of speed straight for Victoria and Troy. Before he could warn her, the sheer blurring speed and powerful thrust gives a blinding point of impact with Victoria's Experimental Unit Fighter. She didn't know to brace for impact which jostles Victoria unforgivingly within her cockpit. Like a slow drunkenly-romantic dance does her fighter float apart and away from Troy's against the moon's light gravity. Troy lands just a few feet from Victoria at the edge of a large crater. The strong impact from Tenam leaves

Victoria slamming and bouncing from the moon's surface like a ragdoll.

She can hear her breathing mixing with the panic-y chatter of her squad. Her senses have become dazed. Victoria's sight blackens and then slowly reappears. She can't get a fix on her bearings or the reality that she is lost to her squadron, Bravo team. "Troy . . ." Victoria says sweetly. "It's beautiful." Commander Tenam and his remaining squad gather around Victoria's downed unit fighter, found planted firmly on its back. They now listen to Victoria who is talking to herself while Alpha teams' shuttle daringly leaves the moon's surface along with the remainder of Bravo team. Victoria can see the ship's launch in her field of vision. She says before losing consciousness, "The stars are . . . beautiful . . ."

Troy, Victoria, Laura, Jane, and Darren chose to play God by delivering judgment upon the people of the Earth for whatever the cause. Whether it was for a righteous end or a self-important mark shall start the beginning of the end with another declaration of war unofficially signed and sealed once again in blood. A savage war not seen since men and women referred it to a civil war that which divided families and questioned faiths.

For the Nations of Earth they will only witness the Devoir-Con aggression as a fire in their garden of territorial held worlds. As for Devoir it has been agreed upon by the

Pride Systems to begin a blitzkrieg offensive to take the Earth held worlds in desperation because of the 20 year war aftermath. There will be many iron horsemen that will come far and wide seeking an end. As for Susan Kempt: Her rider is pale.

Susan arrived not too shortly back on Xiston where she traveled from the capital city, Soul, to an island just South. The hover craft ride over the calm waters seemed longer and colder than the first time she has been there. She was summoned by the Ecologist Faction by a letter found under her room door at the old outpost. The hover craft pilot accompanied Susan from behind when they arrived on the shore. He is clearly an agent. Though he seems young, Susan thinks he is easily persuaded like she was.

Past the trail that Susan and the agent walked is an abandoned construction yard. For Susan it is a familiar sight for vermin to meet. She walks further in as her escort watches on expressionless. Susan Kempt comes into the corner of a rusted and broken down dozer. She stops to look around the high ridges and cliffs surrounding the area. She then looks on ahead where a man walks out of a clearing towards Susan. Susan folds her arms about her chest and leans against the dead dozer machine to appear calm. Her body language comforts the man enough to come closer with a hanging broad smile upon his face.

"Welcome, Susan." said the man. "We've been expecting you." "Yeah," Susan said calmly, "it's been a long time coming." With every step he takes, Susan's heart seems to beat louder and louder.

Susan boldly moves away from the dozer and closes the gap between her and the mysterious man. At just a foot away, Susan notices a small cordless ear-piece in the Ecologist's ear. Aside from the hover craft pilot, she knows there are likely more agents within range of the meeting. Susan realizes she has no choice now. The Ecologist agent's smile slowly turns to a frown when he sees a pistol being pulled from underneath her coat at him. Susan then grabs the man and swings herself behind him as if he is a shield. Suddenly Susan's dumbfounded escort, who is farther from the two, begins to reach clumsily under his coat. It is obviously for a weapon. Susan fires a single round that strikes the man in the leg thus causing him to fall to the ground in a scream of pain.

"What is the meaning of this?!" asked her captive in a panic. Bluntly Susan expresses, "Survival. Now call off your dogs. I wasn't even trying to aim at that idiot!" The agent swiftly agrees, "Alright. Alright! Sniper teams disengage the target." Susan can see movement above and amongst the ridges. As she suspected this area is more alive than first imagined. "Now what, Susan?" asked the man in a patronizing tone. Susan Kempt answers harshly, "We're moving out of here." Slowly with the gun to his back, Susan escorts the Ecologist agent towards the path she previously walked on.

"Look around you, Susan. We are everywhere. You will never get away with what you've done." Spat the agent. "So you planned on killing me like the boy?!" Susan argued. The captive agent replies, "Boy? That *boy* was raised in madness. He's no better than a weapon. It was you who failed to convert General Armada's Special Unit Zero into a soldier for *our* cause. And don't you remember our cause, Miss Kempt? To take down Devoir-Con and put an end to war." Susan says in anger, "He's a 14 year old that was made into a victim by unknown forces that pulled him from right to left by the evils and ideals of both sides. You and the Ecologists are cowards."

"You've gotten too close to him, Susan. Your love is a testament to your weakness." told the mysterious agent. She finally comes to the path that will lead to the hover craft. "On your knees." Susan demanded. He hesitantly complies; feeling the soft ground with his palms thinking it may be his last time. She says, "Now you know how it feels to be as helpless as Cero. To consistently be in your enemy's sights." "A storm is coming." said the agent. "A storm, Susan. I promise there will be fire, ice, and a hail unlike anything seen before.

It will scream down on you and Armada's heads." "Close your eyes." Ordered Susan who now finds herself struggling with her humanity. A short time passed before the Ecologist agent opens his eyes. Susan is gone and the only remnant of her is the sound of the hover craft leaving across the waters.

And as for what is left of Bravo team, just a few hours have passed within the large Systems Shuttle. Jane is endlessly weeping. For Jane, the failed mission is a living tragedy. She couldn't hold the tears any more. Within a small and dark room does she hold the personally felt shame of seeming weak. She, of all people, knows what General Song and Devoir are capable of. Jane has nothing to come back to and nothing to lose.

Outside Jane's door Laura can hear soft and quiet sobbing. She opens the door in curiosity which floods the room with pure light. Jane looks away. "I'm sorry." told Laura. "I wasn't thinking." Before Laura turns away, Jane gestures for her to come in. While wiping the tears from her face, Jane asks, "If you're truly my sister, than what is your story?"

Laura walks further in towards the bed that Jane is sitting on. "I'm a soldier." said Laura. Jane shakes her head with her eyes staring off into nothing and says, "No. Not like me." Laura probes, "Then what?" Jane answers, "Like many scattered and lost children during the 20 year war I was filtered into a government established disciplinary school during most of my childhood. That is until I was adopted and raised by a former Devoir-Con soldier named John Estochin. I guess you can say that he taught me the old romantic era of war and peace with stories of his past. I've been hearing it until my adulthood."

Laura questions, "A former soldier?" Jane wipes her tears and once again answers, "Yes. And so was I. At the age of 17 the war ended. But being as stubborn as I am I later signed on as a Panther pilot as soon as I was 18 just a year later. Protecting the weak and dying civilians of Tinota from Pirate Scavengers and thieves was an honor. Especially since I was following in my Father's foot-steps. Yet things are never that simple. The original dwellers of Tinota, known as the Terrors, threatened the human colonies for their own survival which was due to the fallout of the war. It was my Father's heart that chose to be a mercenary and Terror sympathizer. Imagine that. And for him I betrayed my Panther squadron and Devoir-Con forever. Now they have him, Laura. This mission was everything. Everything to me."

Laura almost couldn't believe everything she heard coming from the lips of her twin sister. She gives a long pause filled with questionable thoughts. Thoughts about what was told to her by her long time mentor, Sarah Ward. Now what

Sarah told her sounds like a warning. That the Pride Systems may not be what they say they are.

Laura opens up honestly, "Civility, independence, and pride. That is what I was taught for 18 years in an institutional class room. I was told just a few days ago that when I was a baby I was a complete unknown when I arrived to Chariot. 'No known Mother or Father to claim except a missing twin sister. I was a good soldier myself. I chose to be a Chariot Warrior pilot. I maintained peace, like you, against Pirate Scavengers during the 9 years after the war."

"And how is your loyalty?" asked Jane as she once again rubs her moist face. Laura says again with guilty-searching jade eyes, "I'm truly sorry . . . about your . . ." "Loss?" said Jane who easily finished her twin's broken sentence. "I haven't lost anything. Not until I am buried after clawing a deep scar on all three Pride System worlds. And they will forever know me as the Scourge of Tinota."

Darren walks in on Jane and Laura in a huff and says, "It's the General. General Armada was responsible for sending the unknown unit fighter that attacked us and the Nations of Earth forces." "What?!" questioned Laura in a shout. "That can't be. Then what was the point of all that? We just lost two of our squad leaders!" Jane says coldly, "Don't be foolish, Laura. If this is true, then your loyalty will only salt your own ground." Darren continues, "I over-heard Alpha team listening to Armada. They're piloting us straight for Xiston where he is waiting." "How many are there of Alpha team?" asked Jane who stands up from the bed she allowed herself to be emotional on. "Three." answered Darren. Jane says, "Good. Laura we need you more than ever. Can I count on you?" Laura tells, "My loyalty has always been what I've said: For civility, independence, and pride. And now I have another real reason to fight: For my family." "Let's move." instructed Darren.

The three Devoir aces walk over to a step ladder that leads strait up to the Systems Shuttle's cockpit-control area. Darren is the first to climb up through the port. The more-than-ready Jane scurries up next followed by Laura.

The control room has an open feel to it. The three Devoir aces' hairs on their heads react to the zero gravity there immediately. The forward windows have automatic shutters attached to them; hiding the brilliance of space from Alpha team. But more important to Jane, Laura, and Darren is a recorded message that their shuttle has intercepted of General Armada.

The message continues on, "-Therefor Cero and the Devil's Son are my main concern unlike those ignorant tools you are transporting. Bring them to me. I'll be waiting here on Xiston where they'll be executed. That is all." Jane couldn't stand for it any longer. To hear a Devoir-Con "pig of an officer" call her an ignorant tool was enough to launch her head first with "claws" fixated on the closest of Alpha team. Suddenly the automatic shutters open fast on each window which gives away her reflection of a mad, floating charge. Her would be prey swiftly clasps her arms and brings Jane's whole body over his head and slams her against the forward control panel. Darren snaps into action as the two other men begin to stand in reaction. "Gun!!!" shouted Laura. "I'm on it!" told Darren. While Darren gets behind the treacherous soldier with the upholstered hand gun, he struggles just a little before he aims the weapon away and at the man who still has Jane bound.

Darren manages to battle and win his finger around the trigger; firing once at the man who is fixated on Jane. Jane quickly reaches for the third Alpha team-mate's holstered weapon and aims it at him. With Alpha team subdued, who has one less living, Laura finally floats further into the control room. "Is he gone?" wonders Laura who comes closer to the motionless gun-shot victim. Even with the obvious corpse lying reclined in his chair and the sound of a gun going off, which is still ringing in everyone's ear, Laura is still in disbelief of what is unfolding before her. She has never witnessed combat and death on such a gruesome and personal spectrum.

And of course the question remains: What's next? With Jane keeping poised on the third Alpha team-mate, the other stops resisting and allows Darren to have complete control of his own weapon. Before tensions rise any further, Darren speaks to the two others belonging to Alpha team, "I suggest you gentlemen sit down. We've got a long ride ahead of us." The two men sit down obediently amongst the chaos of the floating crimson blood that now gels and bubbles from out of the bullet's fatal wound. "Laura," said Darren, "assist Jane in removing that one before he completely bleeds out which will only distract our pilots here." While Jane begins to carry out Alpha teams' dead, she asks Darren, "So where are we headed?" Darren answers, "To Juantan. I know a lot of people there that can hide us until we can figure things out."

What is left of the Devoir aces is just the grit underneath their nails that represents their past and present struggles. Perhaps it wasn't their true hearts they were following. So how does that sum up the destiny of these characters? Where do they find themselves in the next field of battle when love is crossed and desperation fumes the air? For one of the ace pilots, she will choose one over the other. Her fight will take her across the galaxy in a hot pursuit and struggle. Out of desperation she will shape her destiny and the fate of the other Devoir-Con aces.

A day's time has passed within the would-be ill-fated Systems Shuttle that was over taken by the remaining Devoir aces. And Victoria Moore, who is quite alive, finds herself being held captive by the Nations of Earth. With her wrists and ankles shackled, she recognizes she is within a secret military detention center on Earth. She couldn't sleep in her dark cell. Victoria's cell was kept so dark that she hadn't realized if that part of the world was ever night or day. But that doesn't matter to her now. Now she stands before an official Earth Council of Law. These so called representative "lions" of the Nations of Earth sit few in numbers. There council consists of mostly men and one lone female representative. To Moore they and all of the Earth are hypocrites. Truly she has always believed her place within Devoir-Con is rooted with the hatred of the Nations of Earth.

"Victoria Moore, you are being accused of being a terrorist. How do you plead?" asked one of the councilmen. With the thoughts on everything fluttering under her long and dark hair, the councilman's ignorant opening question just reaches Victoria's ears. She answers, "I am not a terrorist. War is upon you and your worlds. And the Earth itself is a prime target." It doesn't matter to her anymore. War is here once again and to tell all feels as comforting as a warm bath. But she'll still have to be convincing for the sake of Troy. And she has a plan.

"We understand that, Victoria Moore." said one who resembles an old crow with thick glasses. "But you and your squadrons' actions suggest the same terrorizing the Nations of Earth has become accustomed to." Another stern councilman impatiently claws out, "Now may we proceed with the hearing? We obviously have more important matters to attend to afterwards." "Wait!" interrupted Victoria. "What about the other prisoner?" "He's still unconscious and in critical condition." answered the young councilwoman. Victoria hushes under her breath, "Then I can save him." "What was that . . . ?" asked the elder in glasses. "I said I can bring them." said Victoria loudly. "'Bring in the rest of my squad here for all of you for judgment."

The stern councilman claws again in objection, "Why would you betray your own soldiers? Why would you betray Devoir?" The councilwoman quickly asks, "What would you want in exchange, Victoria?" "Why would I betray Devoir and what I want are simple." told Victoria. "I want freedom for myself and the other." The entire Earth council swivel their heads into the dark background where they whisper amongst each other. Their calm and stealthy voices turn argumentative. Victoria looks down as if in spite of her dire situation. She is in fact darting her eyes left to right in calculating thoughts of "what if's" and what to expect next from the council.

The council emerges from deep within their "feeding-den"; staring deeply past the spot-light on Victoria Moore. Victoria lifts her head up for an answer. "You'll have your mission, Victoria." told the old crow with the thick glasses. "The sortie will be spear-headed by the one who brought you in: Commander Tenam." She doesn't smile or let the Earth Council of Law know she is pleased with their decision. Instead Victoria keeps reserved. She knows what must be done to keep Troy and herself alive. To maintain her promise to never leave him, Victoria Moore will hunt down the rest of her squadron while weaving past and through war torn galaxies and worlds. And with questions of success over failure swimming in her head, choices will have to be made along with sacrifices unimagined beyond anyone's comprehension.

Except for one: A General named Armada. Armada finds himself back on the world known as Xiston. And here again on the artificial island, he finds himself against a familiar calling. Once again the General is staring through a double plated glass. A reflection of madness glares upon him with sickening thoughts. The hint of alcohol fumigates under his breath that which warms his veins. Armada leans onto the glass while looking down from above at another sarcophagus-like chamber; similar to Unit Zero's. Unknown and uncared for by General Armada, the celebration of 129 years After Ascension is about the peoples' will to reach the stars. It is also to signify the end of the 20 year war.

From General Armada's psyche it is his malicious plan to rebuild from the ashes of the new Earth and Devoir-Con war to form a new alliance with the Nations of Earth behind the distracted backs of the Pride Systems. And from those ashes Armada intends to place himself as a new supreme ruler. With Susan Kempt as his second in command, the General also knows that they will be granted as the heroes who saved the dying worlds of Devoir through this toxic alliance.

It was said once that for 129 years we have really made things complicated for ourselves. Indeed it has been 129 years since we have ascended to the stars and there has been war, famine, and a devil loose beside us. The devil within us all. Yet within what Armada is looking at, the chamber, is another youthful innocent. The child there leaves another sick impression that this young person is like one of his own children. "Sleep." hushed the General. "Sleep well my precious girl, Una."

And Cero: The 14 year old deliverer of men's fates who holds what could have been a key against the Nations of Earth is en route for Xiston where his master, his General, awaits. He finds himself wondering the hijacked Systems Shuttle. Cero suddenly falls to his knees. He places both palms on his very short blonde head from a sudden rush of pain unlike anything he has ever felt before. It can be described as streaks of white lightning clawing at his very mind.

He manages to crawl to a corner beneath a small window before collapsing beneath the stars. Cero then begins to suffer from confusing hallucinations like when he is in his chamber on Xiston; reminiscent of war and Susan Kempt's mind subjugation of peace and an "ideal" humanity. Tears begin to form and then roll down his cheek. He no longer has the control that was bestowed upon him, for the time being, nor can he see the glorious universe in its beauty. It is a power given and a power taken.

A tragedy. A tragedy in the making and a tragedy for all. In the depths of Cero, someone who is bestowed the powers of a "God for rent," he is given the idea of humanities' reality. Through the confusion he is witnessing, Cero is concluding humanities' responsibility to nature and the living universe: People are destructive and un-natural and therefore must all set in their time and be wiped out from existence.

Cero will find himself in confusing places within time as he carries the Ecologist Factions' ideals and General Armada's twisted command and nature. But perhaps there is hope. Only that woman who influenced him can prevent further insanity from constricting them all. Susan Kempt will hold the key, the power, and the heart to stop Cero from destroying himself.